PORTOBELLO
NOTEBOOK

PORTOBELLO NOTEBOOK

ADRIAN KENNY

THE LILLIPUT PRESS
DUBLIN

First published 2012 by
THE LILLIPUT PRESS
62–63 Sitric Road, Arbour Hill,
Dublin 7, Ireland
www.lilliputpress.ie

Acknowledgments to *Cyphers*, where most of
these stories first appeared. Drawings courtesy of Charlie Cullen.

A CIP record for this title is available
from The British Library.

1 3 5 7 9 10 8 6 4 2

ISBN 978 1 84351 202 8

Set in 12 on 16 pt Perpetua by Marsha Swan
Printed in Spain by GraphyCems, Villatuerta, Navarra

To Charlie and Dympna,
good neighbours

Contents

Settling In

SPRING AGAIN. I'm out jogging in the mornings along the canal bank, under the poplar trees opening green and gold, watching my step on the crushed fallen catkins, a purple smear all the way down to the Eveready factory fence. I get my breath, looking across at the Taylor Signs clock – 8.30, the rush-hour traffic just beginning – and I think of Michael sometimes as I jog back home.

THE FIRST TIME I saw him was in the local shop. I was getting the evening paper, to see if my review was in.

He said, 'What's this?' He had a west of Ireland voice, and I looked up. He was holding up a cauliflower. His left side was deformed. Cathy, behind the counter, cutting open the newspaper bundles, said, 'My God, where have you been?' She handed out *Presses* and *Heralds* to people in a hurry, then she said, 'That's a cauliflower.'

He had a long, open smile. 'How do you cook it?' he said, and

I said, 'You just boil it,' and he put it down. He was with a girl, I noticed then. She blushed and muttered something to him, and he said, 'Have you rashers?' Cathy said, 'We have surely,' and she wiped the knife clean.

Cathy was from the North, a newcomer like myself, but already she seemed in charge. It was probably her idea that the shopkeeper give him a job. His left arm bent as if he was carrying a bundle, his left leg bent so that his toe just touched the ground; he used to hang around the door chatting to her. I didn't see him with his girl again. Anyway, he was part of the scene in our street that autumn and winter, pushing the trolley with his good right hand, delivering coal and briquettes. Michael was his name. I got to know him when I bought a piano.

HOW TO HANDLE the enforced idleness small children bring? One of my answers was going to the auction room in Rathmines, as good as a museum to them, and I could lie back on an old sofa, watching paintings, swords, books, mirrors and clocks held up and knocked down: a huge facade, I thought sometimes – when my daughters grew restless and I had to leave – behind which bishops, artists, businessmen and politicians could hide, leaving the rest to do the real, the dirty work, minding children.

'Anyone?' The auctioneer came to a piano, a Victorian box of brass fittings and inlay. There was silence even when he ran his biro down the keys, playing a scale to show that it worked. 'Ah come on. A fiver?' He raised his eyebrows and looked around. Still in the first glow of home-making, and in gratitude for the hour of peace, I put up my hand. He rapped the end of the biro on Middle C. 'Sold!'

When I said, 'Does that include delivery?' he laughed and moved on to the next lot. I stopped at the shop on my way home to ask for a hand.

THAT'S WHAT I think of sometimes in the morning, as I get my breath at the Eveready factory fence: the struggle up to the hall door with that piano, its castors grating on the granite, our hands scrabbling for a hold on the slippery walnut veneer; resting on each step, our backs to the brute, to stop it falling down again.

'Can you play it?' the shopkeeper asked, and when I said No, he said, 'What do you want it for?'

The door opened and my daughters appeared, tiny, remote, staring down at the grotesque thing coming up backwards. Michael said, 'Won't it be nice for the children.' He got a grip with his powerful right hand. 'Let it back to me.'

'I shouldn't have asked you. It must weigh a quarter-ton.'

'You're all right ...' He turned as a handsome girl went by, his own handsome face lighting up like a firefly, fading as she turned the corner.

'You picked a good spot here.' The shopkeeper looked at his watch. 'Come on again.'

'You're settling in?' A neighbour stopped, took off his jacket and hung it on a railing spearhead. A duck and a drake came flying down the street from the canal, quacking courting, six feet above the ground. It was spring. A priest went by. The sun came out and we rested again, backs to the brute.

'Bill's the name,' the neighbour said.

'Adrian.'

'Frank.'

'You have the shop now, Frank?'

'That's me. This is Michael.'

It was like a small party as Michael lifted the lid and slammed a chord.

'And what brought you to Dublin, Michael?'

'The Rehab. I was doing upholstering —'

'She doesn't need upholstering.' Frank nodded at another girl going past, up to the Labour Exchange.

'– But sure I wasn't interested.' Michael looked, and looked away.

'You'll find something. Come on – we'll be here all day.'

Bill rolled up his sleeves and said, 'We'll walk her up.'

Woodworm dust spilled from the squat legs, smearing our hands as we waddled them over the threshold. 'You won't be moving again in a hurry!' Michael smiled as the castors sank into the hall carpet and stopped.

'AND YOU THINK you know someone,' Cathy said, when they found him. She thought he had gone home, back to the west.

It was a week before he came to the surface, floated up swollen, and was seen in the morning rush hour. The blind man was going down Grove Road, beating his white stick along the wall; I was jogging along the other side of the canal as they lifted him out – just by the Taylor Signs clock. That's how you settle in.

Harry

THEIR DAINTY doorknocker rattled, then banged louder. Ta-ta-ta!

'That's Harry,' she said.

'I'm going down to the shed.'

'Shed. Bed. That's all you do.'

'I have to do my work.'

'You're just hiding from life.' His wife's footsteps banged down the hall.

He slipped out the back door and down the dark path to his study, a garden shed. From there he could see Harry come into the kitchen, his hat brushing the white paper lampshade, sending his shadow swinging against the walls. Paring a pencil, he watched him sit down, take off his shoes. He could guess what he was saying – his feet were killing him again. He set to work.

Ta-ta-ta. The Everest typewriter tapped as persistently as Harry, but no door opened. It was like digging granite with a teaspoon. It was like ... he was moaning like Harry. He set to again.

Eight – nine – ten o'clock. For half a page. He didn't dare to reread it. The rest of the book stretched before him like … He turned off the paraffin stove, switched off the light and went up to the house. Harry was on his third pot of tea, drinking it steaming from the saucer.

'Well, Abraham.' He called everyone Abraham.

'Harry. How's the foot?'

'It's both of them. Ooh! My God!'

'You should try another doctor.'

'I've tried every bloody doctor. What do you think it is, ma'am?'

'I don't know.' Through her teeth she said to her husband, 'I'm going to bed.'

'Goodnight, ma'am!'

He took over. 'Another cup of tea, Harry?'

'No, no!'

'I'm making it anyway.'

'I'd love a cup of water if you have it.'

'Is the doctor giving you anything?'

'Everything. It's no use.'

He lived around the corner. Everyone had run from him always. He was odd.

'Not a bad old day, Abraham.'

'Were you out?'

'Just down Pleasants Street, selling a bit of old scrap. Ooh!' He fingered his toes through his socks. 'My God!'

'Is Maurice not here?'

'That fella's never here. I don't know why I took him in.'

He talked as loudly as ever, but he was nervous now. He had begun calling since he had been robbed – two tinkers had broken in, tied him to the bed, beaten him with an iron bar and taken everything.

When half past ten came, he said, 'Are you walking round the corner, Abraham?'

And when they came to his gate: 'Do you want to come in for a minute?'

'No word from the guards?' He stepped in.

'A young fella was round to see me again. What were they like? he says. Like Mother Theresa! I said. What sort of damn fool question is that? Just have a look around, Abraham.'

He went into the sitting room first, as usual. Framed photos everywhere of Jewish men and women in 1920s' clothes; a book – one God ... unity of all things – a prayer book thrown open on an armchair; little ritual cups and bowls in a glass-fronted cabinet – its door still open since the robbery; a piano with rotten legs.

'All right in there, Abraham?'

'All right.'

They stood together in the hall. Maurice's door had been fitted with a big new bolt and padlock. 'Where is he tonight?'

'Shelbourne Park. More trouble than he's worth.'

Maurice was a bookie, but he had been a boxer once. Harry had given him a room, in exchange for protection.

'He looks after himself, that fella. Look what he spent eight pounds on this morning.' Harry led the way down to the kitchen, pointed to Maurice's tins of sardines and jars of pickles on the filthy table. Everything was filthy except the new back door and its gleaming bolts.

'Will I look upstairs?'

'Mind yourself, Abraham.'

The stairs was almost falling down. He went up, close to the wall. On the landing, where the worst drips fell, the boards were sodden. He edged into Harry's small back room.

From its window he could see the back of his own house. His

wife was up again, in the kitchen, tidying after them. She seemed far away. She was right. Shed, bed – burrowing into his never-never memory, dream, imagination or whatever it was. He gave her no life. He felt suddenly as cold as Harry's room.

'All right in there, Abraham?'

A cheap brass ritual candlestick, a wax-splashed matchbox, an electric fire in an oven-roasting tray on the bedside locker. He returned to the landing. 'All right.'

'No harm to put that in.' Harry came up with a light bulb. 'In the front room.'

He hadn't been in there before. In the sudden light the long room seemed unreal: the ceiling sagging like a belly, a brimming red plastic basin under a leak, fallen wallpaper curled like huge ribbons along the skirting-boards, drawers up-ended by the tinkers on the bed.

'This was the mother's room.' Harry clapped his arms about himself for warmth. From the dressing table he took a framed news-paper photo, wiped it on his sleeve, screwed up his eyes and read the caption aloud to himself. 'Rabbi Hertzog … That's the uncle.'

'Where's he?'

'Manchester. That's where he was.'

'You never thought of following in his footsteps?'

'God no.' He put it down carefully. 'I stayed with the mother.'

Standing under the bare swinging light bulb, listening to Harry talk about his mother, he thought of his own mother, a woman who had only to stand at a bus stop for someone to appear and tell the story of his life. He had it too; he must have got it from her. What was it?

'… Never spit in somebody else's water, she used to say. You might have to drink from it someday …'

He nodded. Some sort of passivity? He seemed to have spent

half his life like this – in pubs, trains, under trees along the canal bank – listening.

'Where's that fella got to?' Harry broke off and went to the window.

'He'll be here.'

'What time is it at all?'

'It's only eleven.'

Harry began to talk again – stories about his horse and cart, long-ago journeys through Ireland, buying feathers, lead, antiques, scrap.

Listening … like a cracked jug that never filled … he looked over Harry's sloping shoulders at the chaos. A gilt plaster pediment torn from a mirror, crowned with a lead cherub in an overcoat of greasy fluff. A broken violin stained with ox-blood boot polish. A tiny picture lay on the littered dressing table. He took it up.

Why? Some basic flaw? Still listening, he licked a finger, dabbed at the paint. His fingertip turned black and he licked another finger, dabbed again until he saw white; green. He turned it to the light. A white waterfall, a green field below with two goats and a figure the size of a pin, its head picked out with one grain of red. 'That's lovely,' he said.

'What's that?' Harry took the painting, screwed up his eyes again, turned it over – the old dealer for a moment – and tapped its back. 'That's on board.'

'You don't want to sell it?'

'I'd give it to you, only it's not mine.' Harry set it down, went to the window and peered out again. 'Everything's between me and the sister, above in Kimmage Road West.' He walked down the room, clapping his arms about himself again. He made an effort, picked up the ruined violin. 'Now that's something. That's worth a fortune …'

There was a scraping noise, like a rat, he thought. But it was a key turning in the hall door's new Chubb lock. Harry went first, limping quickly downstairs, calling, 'Is that you, Maurice?'

'Who do you think it'd be, you cunt?' Back from the dog track, his leather bag clutched to his leather overcoat, Maurice brushed past them both. His face lead-grey, flabby jowls scowling, he was like an anti-Semite cartoon. He unlocked and unbolted his door and disappeared.

'About that picture ...' Harry opened the hall door, talking loudly, as if to hear his own voice one last time that night. 'That'll be all right. I'll be seeing the sister on Sunday. She won't be too hard on you.'

'Will you be all right now?'

'Goodnight, Abraham.'

He walked home slowly around the corner. All the nights he had walked home. He looked up at the stars. All the stories he had heard. He walked up the steps. Strange how his life had taken shape. He raised the knocker; a small brass mermaid holding a scallop shell of brass, then remembered he had the key.

'Ssh,' his wife called up softly as he shot the bolt.

Seeing things ... hearing things ... trying to write things. That would be his life, as Harry's life had been buying junk and trying to sell it on. There would be no change now. He felt a spasm of sadness, almost like a pain.

From the kitchen he saw Harry enter his bedroom and, framed for a minute in his curtainless window, undress to his shirt and Sabbath skullcap. The light went out and he disappeared, alone now with his gangrened feet and those words neither of them had ever spoken – 'hardening of the arteries'.

Strange how that picture had been there all the time amongst that rubbish. And now it would be his. He tiptoed downstairs, looked into the children's room, went into his own.

His wife murmured, 'Is he all right?'

'Maurice came home.' He undressed.

'Poor Harry,' she sighed. The row was over.

He got into bed beside her. He could see it, even in the dark. The white waterfall pouring down, the red-capped figure minding two goats in the green below. His wife turned on her side, and he heard her deep breathing – asleep already, now he was home.

He would try harder. He would live, he would give. He'd begin in the morning. He put his arm about her, and fell asleep too. Such a beautiful picture.

Going Back

I KNEW HIM from somewhere. About fifty. A brown pinstripe suit, the tongue of a worn brown leather belt hanging from under the waistcoat; shoes the same dark orange as his hair, the big freckles on the backs of his big hands. He flipped a suitcase like a matchbox onto the luggage rack, lay back in the seat and rested an arm about his daughter's neck. She was about eighteen, so beautiful that I couldn't lift a finger to the No Smoking sign when he took out his cigarettes.

She shrugged off his arm and took a book from a hessian bag, blue-embroidered Virgo. He looked out the window in an agony of boredom as the first fields of County Dublin appeared, turning to his daughter as she slipped off her shoes and tucked bare feet up behind her blue-jeaned bottom.

'Warm enough, love?' He cupped a bare foot with his hand. She wriggled it off irritably, didn't look up from her book. He turned to me in desperation. 'Don't they have no heating on these trains?'

'It probably takes a bit of time to get going.'

He pressed his hand to the grille below the seat. 'Freezing. Then they wonder why the tourists is falling off.' He took out his cigarettes again. 'Smoke?'

'Thanks.'

He sat forward, elbows on knees, his strong face a foot from mine. 'And what about the North then?'

'What do they make of it in England?'

'Every night on the telly. Then there's the economic situation. What's petrol over here now? Ooh it's got dear here. Two cups of tea and two sandwiches in the Buffy – what was it, love, four-fifty?'

'Mm.' She glanced at me, frowned and went back to her book.

'You're on holidays?' I said.

'Jackie –' he turned to her again with a smile, '– she saw this Getaway Special Offer. Of course it's not so bad for us what with the sterling situation ...'

'You like Ireland?' I tried to draw her into the conversation, but he was there before me again, one hand brushing a speck from her peasant-weave shirt.

'Anything old, she likes it. Not like Trace, she's like her Mum. Smoked glass, Scandinavian steel – that's her, eh love?'

She nodded, staring in concentration at the page. He glanced at his watch, cleared his throat, and tapped his toes on the floor, looked at me and said, 'Wonder if there's a bar on these trains?'

I sat still as he got up. 'Hang on,' he said, and as he went out I placed him.

'Where are you going to?'

She looked up at once; shut the book, smiling as she told me. I was right. 'Same here,' I said.

'Really?' A beautiful smile. Rose lips half-parted, wide-apart eyes.

She had taken my question as the opening of a conversation, so I said, 'What are you reading?'

'Fine Art. I'm at Salford –'

'No, I mean –' Even as we laughed, I found myself glancing over her shoulder at the door.

'Oh, this?' She turned her book face-up. The Pre-Raphaelites. She opened it again and resumed reading as her father appeared, his hands full with two cans of beer, a can of Coke, three packets of crisps. 'Only cheese and onion, love.'

'Mm-mm.' She took them without looking up.

He handed me a can, snapped open his own. 'Cheers.'

'Thanks. Cheers.'

Tap-tap of his shoes on the floor. He pressed his hand again to the heater, shook his head, looked at me. He didn't remember me. I risked it.

'Your daughter was saying that you're going to –' I mentioned the station.

'You know it then?'

'Not really.' I lied into his eyes. 'I'm just visiting.'

'Same as myself. I haven't been back this long while.'

'That's where you're from?'

'A few miles out of the town. Lavally. You wouldn't know it.'

I shook my head. I was right. Liam was his name.

I WAS THE LITTLE Lord Fauntleroy then, a younger, boy version of this princess by his side. I spent my holidays with an aunt in Lavally. Liam helped about the place that summer, earning his fare to England. He cut and footed the turf, burnt the furze on the ditches, mowed thistles. He was seventeen; I was a few years younger. I have three memories of that summer.

The first. One day my aunt sent me down to the bog with a

bottle of tea and a sandwich for Liam. Before bringing back the bottle, I had been given a drag of his cigarette. He had gone on smoking the butt, holding it between his black nails until there was only the red tip. Then he had gone down into the cutaway bog, calling to me as he pulled down his trousers, 'Do you want to see it coming out?'

Appalled, I had stood as far away as I could and watched an orange banana of excrement slide out. 'Now let me see yours,' he said, but I could produce only a pale comma. Then I had washed my hands in the bog hole and dried them with sedge. Liam had spat on his hands and taken up the slane again.

HERE I WAS, a middle-aged man sitting opposite him, knees to knees in the train, and I couldn't introduce myself. Everything I remembered him by was unspeakable.

THE NEXT. Was he burning furze or mowing thistles? Anyway, it had begun to rain.

'Hi! Stand in out of that!' He backed into the ditch under the bushes, his hands on my shoulders, looking out over my head at the downpour. 'And may it never stop,' he said. Branches cracked behind him as he backed further into shelter and lit one of his precious Woodbines, offering me a drag if I sang him a song. I sang something I'd heard on the radio:

'"She was only sixteen, only sixteen, and I loved her so
But she was too young to fall in love, and I was too young to
    know ..."'

'That's all I know,' I said.
'Good man yourself.' He gave me the drag.
'Now you sing.'

'Sure I've no song.' He stood looking out at the rain, talking about England, and how he'd be off in the autumn. And then — the second thing I remembered, as clearly detailed as one of those Pre-Raphaelite paintings his daughter was gazing at now — 'Come here till I show you.' He had backed deeper into the bushes, so we were in a hut almost of furze and hawthorn, where he opened his trousers and released a large sallow cock that sprang up rigid. He pulled a handful of ivy and woodbine off the ditch and handed it to me. 'Give me a stroke of that.'

Timidly I had taken the strands and brushed them across his cock.

'Arra, do it right.' Taking the ivy and woodbine whip, he had lashed down at himself. 'Like that. Or will I do it to you?'

'No, no.' Frightened by that, I had given a few stronger strokes, and the cock swelled and rose still more, but he was not satisfied.

'Go on, hit it can't you.'

What would have happened if the rain had not stopped then and the sun shone out again? And seeing that I would whip him no harder, he had buttoned up his trousers and let me out into the field.

LEANING FORWARDS, elbows on knees, beer can in one hand, cigarette in the other, he was chatting about the Pakistanis now, and the Blacks. He said the black man was a fine man, but the bloody Paki would live in your ear. His daughter stared unblinking at her book as she turned a page. I thought of my last memory of him.

IT WAS THE END of my summer holidays and I was going back to school. The train was crowded with men going back to England, so I had to stand in the corridor in pools of spilt Guinness and tobacco spit. Ballinlough ... Ballymoe at each small station — we were shooting back through them now, each closed up, derelict – another small crowd of men was waiting, filling the train even more.

Then – 'I think you could squeeze in beside me' – a terribly familiar voice: Father Burke, my Latin teacher at school. He was coming back from holidays too, from further west. He moved and made space for me, I had sat down before I noticed Liam sitting opposite. He was with some older men and gave me only a nod, then returned to listening to their stories – of landladies in Sparkhill, of blankets so thin that a sneeze lifted them to the ceiling; of a man offered onions every evening for his tea until he said, 'Ma'am, I don't eat fruit.' Their laughter stopped as we approached Athlone. The men stood up seriously and made to reach down their cases, calling to Liam, 'Are you right? Come on, hurry up!'

'What?' Liam jumped up.

'Holyhead. They don't waste time over here, boy. The train only stops a minute in Holyhead.'

The train rolled over the Shannon. Liam stood, one hand white-tight on the handle of his case, staring down at the dark wide river and bobbing boats.

'You're over now, Liameen!'

His face blazed red as he reached for the door-strap, and as the train pulled into Athlone station he sprang out onto the platform. 'Lads! Lads! Hurry on, we're landed!' he called in another window to friends from home.

'I think they're pulling your leg,' Father Burke murmured, but it wasn't until the whistle blew, when someone shouted, 'Get in, you bloody *amadán!*' that Liam understood and came back into the carriage. That was my last memory of him, for Father Burke had brought me with him to the dining car, where we spent the rest of the journey.

ALL I WANTED to ask about the past thirty years in between, and couldn't. He looked at me, his face innocent of the knowledge I had; then looked at his daughter, and her beautiful eyes still fixed on that book. He looked out the window, tapped his toes, looked at his watch, and drank the last drops of beer.

'My round,' I said. I stood up.

'Ta!' He almost sprang to his feet. 'Does you good to have a bit of a chat, eh?' He looked down at his daughter. 'I'll be in the dining car, love, if you need anything.' He led the way along the corridor. I nodded a smile at his treasure child, turned cold as I got back an adult's smile of complicity, a raising of eyes to heaven. Then I went down to the dining car to talk about nothing with Liam.

Mistress

THE COACH STOPPED in the market square, just beside a phone box. The noise of the coach made it hard to hear what she was saying.

'Where are you now?' She sounded as if she was smiling.

'In a phone box in the square.'

'Look out – can you see The Golden Lion?'

'I can.'

'I'll meet you there in half an hour.'

HE WALKED about the town, enjoying the pleasure of waiting. He walked as he had once walked to her flat, but without excited anxiety now. He looked at a Saxon church with a Norman tower, then at a Georgian market house. She had settled in a place very different from Ireland, but walking down the street he passed a pretty thatched house and remembered, tried to remember, a kiss they had had one wet Irish midland morning in the shelter of a thatched gable. He walked back to The Golden Lion, admiring the soft red-brick facade curtained with mauve wisteria. He made a stab at dating it Queen Anne.

He had been on his way home when he decided to visit her. He had spent the last of his English money on the coach fare, and had to buy his drink with a credit card.

'Now, if you'll just give me a swipe of your plastic,' the receptionist said, and he stepped out of the past back into the present.

He sat in a bar darkened by copper pans, stuffed trout and hunting prints, and tried to imagine what she would look like now. He couldn't, any more than he could remember the feeling of that kiss. He could remember her only as she had been the last night they met, fifteen years ago, but he still remembered the way she had sat when he stopped outside her house, the way her skirt had slipped between her parted knees as she sat back in the seat for a moment – then she had stepped out of the car and walked in her gate, not looking back.

'HELL-O.' Her voice was jokey.

He didn't recognize her for a second. She was thinner than she had been, but more handsome. As he stood up he glimpsed a look of envy from the barman.

'Sorry I'm late. The traffic's a bugger.' Her voice was still Irish, but the manner was English.

'Will we stay here? '

'God no.'

He picked up his bag and they went out to her car. She wore stockings and high heels, which had never suited her. Two girls in school uniform coming up the street glanced at them, said, 'Hello, Miss', and hurried past, laughing, leaning against each other, whispering.

Smiling, but leaning away from any suggestion of intimacy,

she got into the car. A shivery grey dog standing on the back seat nuzzled her neck. 'Hello, dear,' she said.

'What sort of dog is that?'

'A whippet.' She tilted back her head against the dog's delicate nose. Her hair was turning grey but the impression was still blonde.

'That's where I teach.' She pointed to the school as she drove out of the town. 'You're not wearing too badly.' She glanced at him as she overtook a lorry.

'Nor you,' he said, and as they cruised past the lorry's long side he studied the way her features had changed, trying to relate them to the face he had known.

'What were you doing in London?'

'I was doing some work in the British Library.'

'Are you famous now?'

'God no.'

She laughed. 'I got fed up with London,' she said.

'You never thought of working in Ireland?'

She shook her head.

'Do you ever go back?'

'Just for a week or two in summer.'

'You never look me up.'

She shook her head again. 'I'm glad you came though. How long have you got?'

'The plane goes at eight.'

'That's OK. There's a nice place to have lunch down here.'

She turned off the motorway and they both relaxed into silence. They had assured each other they could talk easily. He looked out at the tidy Berkshire countryside.

They ate in a pub by a river. The food didn't taste as good as it looked, or the beer, but after lunch he bought two more glasses and they sat outside. There were fat tame ducks on the riverbank and in the shallows.

'How long have you been here?' he asked.

'Eight years now.'

'You must like it.'

'It's all right, if you can stand the people.'

He smiled. 'Anyone special?'

'There is.'

'I'm glad. For long?'

'For a few years now.'

'You might get married.'

She smiled. 'You recommend it, do you?'

'It works.' He put down his glass of beer, so did she, and with the whippet trotting daintily behind they walked along the riverbank. Her high heels caught in the soft turf, so they sat down again by a sluice gate.

'I was amazed when I heard you were married.'

He nodded, and they talked as they looked at the water rushing against the timbers of the sluice gate, eddying back in foamy circles into the river. He thought that if he was with his wife now they would sit in peaceful silence looking at the water, enjoying the warmth of the spring sun and the scent of wet earth and marsh mint. He was about to say that his wife gave him the large lonely space that he craved. He was about to say – She leaves me alone.

'The grass is wet.' She pressed a hand to her skirt and sat up on the sluice gate.

'Do you remember the morning I jumped out of bed?' he said suddenly.

'In Brighton Road? '

'Guess where I went to? I went down to the church.'

She laughed. He felt the warmth of that intimacy he craved,

but wasn't able for. It was as warm, real and simple as the river in the sunshine. 'God, I was screwed up then,' he said.

She made no confession in exchange. He watched a boy and girl walk along the river path, hand in hand. He watched them duck their heads under the trailing leaves of a willow tree, and he looked up at the shape of the big blue-green tree for some consolation.

'That's where I live.' She pointed to a village across the fields.

He felt envy as he looked at a grey spire rising from dark-green trees. 'Does he live with you?'

'Who?' She turned to him.

'Your boyfriend.'

'No. No, he lives in the town.'

His envy settled down and he looked at the Constable landscape and said, 'Will you stay here?'

'I expect so. It's strange, I know more people here than at home.'

'Through the school?'

'And I go out a lot. I play in a quintet now.'

'You still play? '

'More than ever. And I'm singing in the village choir.'

'It sounds like Thomas Hardy.'

'I'm playing over there tonight.' She pointed to the Constable horizon, broken by a giant concrete shape. 'That's the nuclear power station.'

There was less difference now between her humorous and her ironic voice. That was what had changed in her face, he decided – the smile and the frown had become one. It made him thirsty for the intimacy they had once shared.

'You were the first woman in my life, you know.'

'It was very short. A few months.'

'Then I ran away,' he said. He got up from the wet grass. To stop him from sitting beside her on the sluice gate – he thought – she stood up too and they walked back to the car.

'Where did you meet your wife?'

'She was friendly with a girl I was after.'

She laughed again, less ironically, and then shut her eyes to the sun. He took the chance to look at her – her simple stubborn upper lip, her unsuitable clothes. He remembered her long yellow cardigan with the zip, her small breasts and the width of her hips; and his helpless horror as he looked at the thirst he had provoked but could not satisfy – her own helpless frenzy hammering the bed board against the wall, the perspiration glistening on her upper lip.

'Oh that sun is lovely.' She opened her eyes suddenly, caught him looking at her and she laughed openly, naturally. 'How does your wife put up with you?'

Their ease continued as they drove back to her house.

'What's your boyfriend like?'

'In looks? Big forehead. Fair hair – not much on top, but he grows it long at the back.' The ironic jokey tone had returned to her voice. 'He's a doctor.'

'Is he in the choir?'

'No. We go walking together.'

'I hope I'm not –'

'No. We just go away at the weekends. He's married, you see. Here we are.' She stopped outside a pretty terraced house of old dark-rose brick.

He felt dazed as he followed her inside. She went into the kitchen and put the kettle on for tea. Her manner showed that she had wanted to tell him the truth, but didn't want to talk about it. She was a mistress, someone who waited. He stood in the sitting room looking at tastefully spaced objects. Even her violin seemed part of the arrangement. The mantelpiece was bare except for a pale-silver carriage clock. He wished that the hands would turn faster, so that he could be gone, home to his wife.

The Tea Cloth

SHE WAS GOING into her house as he passed by, so he called her name. But instead of just saying Hello, she said, 'Are you coming in for a cup of tea?'

'I won't, thanks.'

'Come on. I want to show you my new work.'

No escape. He followed her upstairs. 'How's Raymond?'

She shrugged her back, turned a Chubb key in the door. 'He's gone.'

'Oh. I'm sorry.'

She turned a Yale key, stepped into her flat, turned on the light. Her hair was dull. There were the first signs of crimp lines in her upper lip. She was like a daffodil a few days after its bloom. She dropped her coat on a chair, sat on it and said suddenly, 'I'm fucked.'

'No you're not.'

'You don't know what it's like out there.'

As he listened, he was working out her age. She had been twenty when he'd first met her ... she'd be forty-two or three now. She breathed out an air of failure, which bored him. She was looking at him as he talked, so he couldn't look at his watch. He looked about the room, as if admiring her paintings. No clock.

She followed his look. 'What do you think?'

'Are they new?'

She got up, and he glanced at his watch. Ten. He'd have to stay at least half an hour.

'These ones are.'

He stood behind her and looked down at the grey roots in her hair.

'What do you think?'

He looked at the pictures. They were almost good. 'They're different,' he said. But he wasn't getting away that easily.

She said, 'I like this one.'

He looked at it. She couldn't draw. She just laid on the paint and hoped it would obey her feelings. He said, 'Where's that? It looks familiar.'

As she told him where, he looked at the pretty little things decorating her room. An old silver inkwell. A da Vinci cherub. That was her idea of art, of life. On the table was a sewing box, and a length of silk she was turning into an arty dress. She loved art; she loved men.

'What did Raymond think of them?'

'He liked these sky studies best.' She moved to another wall and he followed. She stood looking at the pictures, waiting for him to speak. It was the pretentiousness he disliked most, her refusal to simply look at the sky and try to put it down on paper. But she was simple-minded too – she thought art must be different, special, removed from vulgar life. So she chose men who were different, special, removed from vulgar life. But at forty, that type of single man was a drifter. And they left. She turned to him. He looked at one of the pictures. 'I like that cloud.'

'Do you? That's the one he preferred.'

'And still he left.'

'And still he left.' She smiled. 'The bastard.'

'Still, you were together a good while.'

'Only a year.'

'Maybe it was enough.'

'It's not. I can't stand living on my own. You go loopy. You dry up when you're living alone. I need somebody.'

How could she imagine these affairs would last? But her idea remained the same: part-time waitress work in little restaurants, painting in her free time, making nice dinners in the evening, chatting with Raymond about art while she ran up a bolero jacket from a remnant of black satin, then going to bed and making love.

Raymond had run off with a woman who liked watching TV soaps, who didn't object to white sliced bread, who had no fucking sewing box.

'There'll be another. There always has been, hasn't there?'

'It's getting harder.' She led the way to the two armchairs by the fireplace. Her voice wasn't as fey as it once had been. She was becoming what she had despised: ordinary. Her voice was tougher, she spoke naturally, as if simply saying aloud what she thought as she sat alone in this flat at night. 'I'm too soft with my men. I see other women – they nail the guy down, they get pregnant, they take out a mortgage, stop them from drifting off ...' Half joking, but half serious.

He smiled. 'Why not try that next time?'

They had been lovers once, so long ago that the memories had detached. It seemed to him now that it was someone else who had longed for her, waited for her, watched her flirt with smarter boys. She was still the bourgeois bohemian, he thought, her feet planted on the ground, reaching up for the high fruit – drinking with the musician after the concert, going backstage after the play. He wanted to say, 'You're not a painter, forget art, get a guy who has a good job, watch TV together in the evening ...' He didn't, he knew she couldn't change now. She had grown into an idea of herself. Some deep want of confidence, some sense just as deep of being special had turned her into this tight-skinned, thin, lonely woman staring straight ahead at middle age.

He looked at his watch – only a quarter past – as she got up again, to make tea, to prolong his stay. She set out a dainty cream china teapot in the shape of a seashell, a Georgian sugar spoon. The wind rattled the window. Absently, she took an old, stained tea cloth and twisted it roughly like a rope, then wedged it between the upper and lower window sashes to keep out the draught. Looking at her pursed lips, he could imagine her talking to herself when she was alone. The phone rang.

'Hello ... no. Just a friend ...' She turned her back to him.

He looked out at the moon cutting through grey cloud.

'... OK.' She put down the phone. 'That's him.'

'Raymond?'

'He wanted to know was I alone. He wants to call around.'

'Where's his new woman?'

'She's away. He said he's lonely. He wants to talk.'

He stood up. The sadness of it wiped out his relief to be escaping.

'There's no rush.' She sat down. 'Take your tea.'

He played his part, sat talking for half an hour, to make Raymond a little jealous. Her face took on colour. When he kissed her cheek goodbye her eyes were bright. Down in the street, he looked up at her flat, and saw a light come on in the bedroom. She would be tying some piece of rose silk about her neck, preparing for battle. Then he thought of the stained, twisted tea cloth, her pursed lips as she wedged it down between the sashes – the first crude, real and simple thing he had ever seen her do.

She might win yet. Anything was possible. He looked up at the moon, sailing free across the sky, and felt suddenly jealous as he walked home.

Saturday Evening Mass

AS HIS MOTHER grew old she went out less often. She took a taxi to the doctor, the hairdresser, the chiropodist. On Saturday evenings he drove her to Mass. When he had told her, twenty-five years ago, that he no longer went to Mass, she had cried as she had cried when her own mother was dying; helpless tears. Now she accepted it as a cranky form of independence, as she accepted her swollen knuckles, living alone, or the tablets she had to take for her heart.

He reached into the back seat for the rug, the old plaid they had used to sit on at picnics, and she laid it on her knees. She noticed a darn in it, and he explained that his wife had mended a tear their children had made. She rubbed the darn with the backs of her fingers, making it woolly so it blended with the rest, and said her mother had taught her that. What once might have bored or irritated him brought peaceful warm conversation now. Since her husband had died she had found her own little ways of independence. She didn't go out because she didn't want to. She wore what was comfortable – a man's quilted green jacket over her cardigan this evening, and a threadbare bit of silk to hide her withered neck. Once so timid and genteel, a countrywoman uneasy in this bourgeois suburb, now she spoke her mind more easily, said what was spontaneous.

'Look.' She nodded at the two old bachelor brothers out walking their Scottie dog.

'Look at them talking. You'd think they hadn't met for years.'

'The heavenly twins,' he said, and she laughed.

He drove down the wide road between the lime and chestnut trees, turned right at the traffic lights. She looked in the gourmet grocery shop window at the checkout girls.

'Can you see Pauline?'

'There, at the end.'

'I see her, the blonde mop. We'll stop on the way home. Remind me to get the *Guide*.'

Her routine of Mass and shopping no longer smothered him; approaching death had set it in a wider frame. He drove under the black-stone railway bridge, turned right again up the narrow road of red-brick houses between cars parked bonnet to boot on either side. He had to stop in the middle of the road. 'I'll be back in an hour.'

'Do you know what you could do – go up to the park and get me a few sticks for the fire. I love the smell of them.' She folded the rug and put it on the back seat, then she put her feet out awkwardly on the road, muttering, 'I'm like a giraffe.' The way she walked slowly to the porch, dipped her bent fingers in the holy water and blessed herself made even the big crude granite church seem beautiful. It made him want to park the car and follow her inside. But he had tried that, and found it still led back to the enclosed world he had escaped. He had to forage for scraps outside. He took short cuts up the familiar old roads, past the park – that cranky independence – down to where the river flowed between a playing field and a steep wooded slope.

The smell of half-dead water and the damp sandy clay brought memories. As he walked upstream, he remembered the children from the flats swimming in their mothers' saggy bloomers in summer time; a day he and his brother had invited them home, and his vague uneasy feeling that something was wrong as the children had trooped upstairs. He stood to watch a heron in the shallows. The memories flowed past like the river. He looked at the heron's grey shoulders and yellow-streaked breast, the water sliding by its long pale-brown legs, the purplish alder and light-green willow trees reflected in the surface, all as still as the pale-blue evening sky. It was like a glass pane. On the other side, in death, he would be there. He felt no fear, instead a peaceful joy. Breathing in the feeling, reverent as his mother returning from Communion, he walked back slowly to his car.

THERE WAS a cheer from the playing field. A soccer match had ended. Two teams of middle-aged men were making for the ship's container used as a changing room. The few people along the touch lines were straggling away. He glanced at one of them – head hunched, hands cupped, taking a light for a cigarette from another. He hesitated, but then Tom glanced up and saw him, and he crossed the rough wet grass.

'Tom. Where did you spring from?' It came out wrong, the wrong tone in his voice. Quickly he held out his hand.

'I saw you passing – I was thinking it was you.' Deliberately slowly, Tom put his cigarette between his lips, then shook hands. His face opened, then it was cold again. He turned to the man beside him and said, 'I'll see you,' and the man walked away.

'A long time.' He got the sweet smell of beer from Tom's breath. 'Where have you been?'

'Thailand. Did I not send you a card?'

'When did you get back?'

'There a few months ago.'

'And where are you staying?' Already he was watchful.

'In a hostel. '

He didn't reply. Tom picked up his unease, and as if well used to that he withdrew into silence. Together they walked down to the river and stood looking at its silent swift flow. An electric-blue flash, a kingfisher, flew upstream.

'You always see something if you stand still.'

'I do plenty of that.' His Munster accent rippled through the standard tone.

How had he become a drifter? How had someone with the pick of beautiful girls when he was young ended up alone? At a distance, he knew the answer. At odds with his father, Tom had left home as a boy, and now his parents were dead he drifted like the twigs and leaves on the river. It was still in his face: the unforgiving look of someone who had known narrow country ways. But as always when he was with him, that answer failed. It was more than that. Tom was as determined in his own way as he. Drifted, maybe, but so had the bog-water trickles and mountain streams that formed this river. He was a man in his own right.

'Which way are you going?'

'I have to collect my mother from Mass.'

'Have you time for a drink?' Tensed like a cat, ready to go at the first hint.

'Just a quick one.' He looked at the thin yellow face, the dark hollows under his eyes, the thin-rimmed glasses, the grey hair sleeked and slightly too long at the back, the beautiful hands. His fingertips moved all the time against his thumb, as if cleaning them. The sleeves of his jacket were too long.

They walked together up to the road, then down to join the riverbank again. In the calm taut water above the fall, a cormorant surfaced, its bill tilted like a bayonet, its black back shining like oil.

'Look at him.'

'I saw him earlier, with an eel as big as himself.'

'I bet you it didn't get away.'

Tom smiled. 'It didn't.'

'Do you ever see any of the old crowd now?'

'Strange, I ran into Terry Hunt. He asked me to dinner.'

'I heard he was home. Nice place?'

'I never got there. He had some appointment.' Watching the cormorant sail high in the water, Tom added — that smile again, 'We had a burger in McDonald's.'

He led and Tom followed without question down the path to the foot of the fall, where they watched the foaming water settle and run smooth.

'What's the hostel like?'

'OK. You have your own room.'

'No girlfriend?'

'Here? Are you joking?'

'Any jobs coming up?'

'I don't want one. I'm tired of it.' Tom's eyes fixed on the river, following its flow down to a bed of gravel, where it broke into rough white again.

He knew that life; he had tasted it once when they had worked together abroad. The novelty-excitement energy, endless as the river — teaching English all day, drinking and talking all night — art, politics, religion, sex — until his throat was raw. He had come home, refreshed; Tom had gone on – Bahrain, Bangkok, always further east. He had rung late one night a few years ago, drunk: 'I'm in bed with a beautiful girl. Her name's Nag. Do you want to talk to her?' There was rustling, sighing, and then a sleepy girl's voice had said, 'Hello.' Since then there had been silence.

'And what'll you do?'

Tom shrugged. In his silence he could hear the cry: Take me home. They stood to watch the cormorant bob past on the fast water and vanish under the bridge. Together they walked along the path to the pub's car park.

Tom led the way inside, as easy as the cormorant in the river – and as alert. He glanced down the counter, saw the man he had been with at the football match, and coldly turned away.

'What'll you have?'

'Just a glass.'

'That'd only bother you.' Tom called for two pints. His beer went down as always in half a dozen swallows.

'Why not do one last stint abroad? A few years in Saudi, and you'd have enough for the deposit on a flat.'

'I can't stand Saudi.'

'Were you there? You didn't save?'

'I used to go to Thailand for the holidays.' The line, deep as a weal on either side of his mouth, tightened about his smile. Aloneness surrounded him, like the static light when you pull off a shirt in the dark.

So long he had been doing it, so long. The drive always longer than expected, from the airport to the new school. The bare newly cleaned apartment. The first-night drink. Then the first classes, the front-row pupils well reared and ambitious. The troublemakers sat in the middle, yawning. The slow ones sat at the back, smiling and hiding from the light. The weak were nice, the strong were not

– life was so simple a child could understand it. Then suddenly it was the end of term: parties, students queuing to take his photo and ask for his address. And never writing. And the faces he had grown used to fading, and in a month forgotten. And then Tom was home to Ireland, where he had no home, which drove him abroad again.

He glanced at his watch as he raised his glass, preparing his escape. Tom saw the look and reached into his pocket again. 'One more.' He stood an inch too close.

He could feel his loneliness, like the chill when you open a fridge door. 'I can't, Tom. My mother will be waiting.'

'Won't she be lighting candles for a while?'

'Here.' He put some money on the counter. As he left, he saw the man at the end of the counter glide down to sit beside Tom. His guilt cleared. He knew they would be there till closing time. Who cared about art, politics, religion, sex? Any talk would do, talk and drink, until they were on the warm wave, drifting away from it all. Tom would drink until he was speechless and could only gesture, and then even his hands would be still.

Outside it was almost dark. He made his way along the path by the murmuring river and up by the waterfall's roar – then he stopped. He couldn't leave him like that. Say he brought him back to his mother's for an hour? He could see it through Tom's eyes: helping with the shopping of an old woman who was taking him home. Home: a place where a fire was kept alight always, a place where you could be tender, off guard. She would sit him at the fire, built up before Mass and burning bright now. No, he wouldn't take a drink. Would he like tea? And a boiled egg? How did he like it? And the face, hardened by years in foreign-teacher compounds, by mean jobs and cheap affairs, would open into a boy's smile and say, 'Just getting firm, thanks.' He would look up at her as she poured the tea, look at everything – the holy pictures and photos on the mantelpiece, the pink knitted egg cosy and the striped knitted tea cosy, the small buttered slices of homemade bread, the little knife with the blackened bone handle and the tea spoon she had taken from the Great Southern Hotel – like a stranger in a foreign land.

He couldn't – if he did that, Tom would never go. He couldn't – any more than he could go with his mother to Mass. He went on walking up the muddy path. Startled, the heron rose from the shadows, flapping its big grey silent wings, its long legs trailing as if broken, giving its cranking cry as it glided through the yellow light spilling from the pub windows, and dropped out of sight again. As suddenly he saw the evening ahead: leaving his mother at the gate, sitting for a minute in the car until she was inside, and then driving away. As he went he gathered dead sticks, a withered bough of ivy that would burn with sweet smoke for her that night.

The Cricket Match

SOMETIMES on summer evenings he walked up to the cricket ground, a place where he could sit and think. Anyone could go there but few did unless there was a big game – when the West Indies played, it had been like a rock concert, with girls crowding about the big dusky stars. This evening the benches were empty. A few members sat outside the pavilion, drinking beer. He walked around the boundary rope to where the sun shone longest, down by the chestnut trees. Swifts, those birds that do not like the country, skimmed screaming over the surrounding rooftops. Beyond were the Dublin hills, green rising into blue. The town-hall clock struck a quarter hour in its grave tones. As a boy he had heard it from his bed at night. In the end he hadn't moved far.

The groundsman stood to chat about the dry weather ... sparrows pecking fibre from the boundary rope. There was a shout from the wicket – the middle stump was down. The umpire raised his finger, and a batsman made the lonely walk. One of the fielders lay on his back, arms outspread. The others stood in a white huddle while the next bat padded up.

'Who's playing?'

'The Thirds and Westmeath.' The groundsman strolled on.

The new bat hacked the crease and took his stance. Someone said, 'Bill,' and threw the ball to a middle-aged man with his shirt collar standing up at the back. That, the name, the way he slowly raised his hand, and the ball sprang straight into it as if attached to an elastic; the way he ran up on slow tiptoe, the slow leg-break he bowled – they made the man on the bench sit up and watch the game.

AS HE APPROACHED the school a canal ran alongside the road – the same canal that went through the city he had left far behind. He stopped the car and sat on the bank, looking at the still water, then he lay on his back looking up at the sky. He was twenty-three, which seemed old to him. He was going to his first job. As he drove on he looked at cottages and farmhouses scattered in the fields, thinking that soon he would know the names of the people who lived in them. He couldn't believe it.

One of his aunts had lent him her car, a duck-egg blue Renault. She said she didn't want it. She wanted to be free to drink, he knew. He had the anxious innocent face of someone half unaware of what he knew. At the interview he had agreed to teach French and take games – cricket in summer, rugby in winter. He would have agreed to anything to get a job in that musty old school behind high stone walls in the middle of nowhere, where the world could not reach him. The car rattled over a cattle grid, and he drove up the avenue.

Parents and their children were carrying luggage inside. The headmaster wore an academic black gown, his starched white shirt cuffs flashed as he shook hands and pointed the way. The new teacher went down a dark, flagstoned corridor to a green door. Two young men wearing sports coats and grey trousers like his own turned to look at him as he sidled in. One of them held out his hand and said, 'George Ingram.' The other one said, 'Tom Jacob.'

'Justin Kelly.' He echoed their frank voices.

They stood together awkwardly like strangers in a lift until an old man appeared. His name was Charlie Porter, he taught Latin. His smile, ingratiating and menacing, shifted like his false teeth. He asked where they were from, and when they each said Dublin, he asked, 'What part?' When Tom hesitated, he smiled again. But then a boy came down the corridor ringing a bell, and they went up to the dining hall where the headmaster introduced them and said grace in a fruity voice. The boys sat down at long tables, form by form. As trays of food were served, the older boys spat on the bigger portions, marking them for themselves. Justin thought that soon he would know their names, but again he couldn't believe it. There were almost a hundred of them. It was enough for now to know the teachers' names.

After supper there was Evensong, which as a Catholic he didn't attend. He went up to his room, unpacked his clothes and set his books on a tall window's ledge. For as far as he could see there were big empty fields. Hymn-singing and harmonium music still came from the chapel, but he tiptoed as he went downstairs. Everything smelled old. The floorboards creaked, and the heavy door. It was a warm, silent September evening; rooks were settling in the tops of old trees. He walked down the avenue, and looked up and down the narrow road. There was a ruined Norman tower on a hillside and on another a grey church, like old marks almost rubbed away by time. But as a train's horn sounded and he glimpsed green carriages pulling away across the fields, the cold present returned. He had found his home smothering; he had gone to live abroad, and broken down. This was where his new life would be. The train's horn sounded like mockery.

THE PSYCHIATRIST had given him sleeping pills, which frightened him: they meant he was sick. He hid the small brown plastic bottle under his clothes in the wardrobe and went to bed. As soon as the dormitory lights went out, there was silence as heavy as the air. He didn't wake until a bell rang next morning and prefects called in accents from every part of the country.

The boys sat sleepy-silent at breakfast, filed into the chapel for morning prayer, ran wild for ten minutes around a high-walled yard, then went into school. Justin's class was the first form, half a dozen boys sitting in one corner of a huge, shabby room like a parish hall. There were bars on the windows, cattle were bellowing outside. The blackboard was worn grey, its easel shook on the rough plank floor when he wrote the word *Français*. The boys looked at him and whispered to each other. He taught them the French for Yes and No. When he asked them to say the words, they blushed and laughed. Then slowly they began to talk. Five of them came from the same parish. Their national school teacher had been an old woman who had taught them how to knit.

'Can you all knit?'

'*Oui, oui!*'

He chalked a sentence on the blackboard and asked them to copy it. Some of them wrote well, some badly, but the sixth boy could hardly write at all. 'And he can't knit, sir,' the other five said.

'What's your name?' he asked. The boy looked down at his boots.

'He doesn't know that either, sir.'

'Farr, sir.' He had a western accent that made the others laugh.

'Don't laugh,' Justin said abruptly. They were together at rock bottom.

SO MANY THINGS were strange that to manage he had to set his unhappiness aside. Boys ran away, and teachers not in class were sent to bring them back. One morning it was his turn. He drove along the narrow roads, stopping at gates and looking across the wide fields. Farmers looked at him from their combine harvesters, flocks of pigeons rose from tall brown stubble. He found the boy at last, trotting like a stray dog along the grassy verge. When he opened his car door, the boy got in obediently.

'What's your name?'

'Judd, sir.'

'Are you homesick?'

'Yes, sir.'

'Your parents will visit you.'

Silence.

He learned that some of the boys were orphans, sent to the school by foster parents, whose names they used. The ones the steward called from class to pick potatoes were farmers' sons. When the post came, a prefect shouted the lucky names and flung letters like food into a hungry crowd. Once a week he was on duty and had to call the entire school roll. The names were so strange to him that he found them easy to remember. After a month he knew them all. When they spoke to him, they said 'Sir' in every sentence. They had a shy, obedient manner. They were used to living in their small, enclosed community.

WHEN HE GOT his first month's pay, a cheque for £80, the head-master directed him to a bank in the town, where the manager, a small man with a small, red moustache, came from behind the counter and shook his hand, opened an account and invited him to join the local golf club. Justin went there on his next half-day, played until he was out of sight of the clubhouse, then lay down in the rough and slept. He had thought that to grow up was simply to go away, and all the strands of home — family, friends, religion, school — would turn somehow into a wonderful adult self. Instead the strands had twisted about each other until the twine had snapped, the balloon had drifted away and he had fallen to earth. When he woke, the piercing loneliness and skinless panic of his year abroad were back, like the sleep taste in his mouth. The nodding trees were like giant men. The worst part was the sudden awareness of it, the instinct glimpse that it was not how life need be. The glimpse gone, like the Pole star behind clouds, he returned to the high-walled school.

BUT THERE WAS ALWAYS something new, strange, to absorb him. When his duty day fell on Sunday, to increase its small congregation, he walked the boys down to the grey church. There was the same locked-up smell as in the school. The farmers wore old herring-bone suits; their wives wore old-fashioned hats. They stood as the local landowner, a very fat old man, walked slowly up to the front bench and sat down. Then the service began. A gramophone played a scratched record of organ music and the boys sang. Someone gave him a hymnal, and he joined in. The gloom suited him. He was like a mushroom growing in the dark or a weed growing alone.

Everything was nourishment: the lark's nest of freckled eggs he found in the churchyard when he stepped out during the sermon; the Neolithic knife of white flint he found as he wandered in a vast bog; the loneliness of eating steak and chips in the town on his half-day; even the terror of going to the dance hall on Saturday night. 'Go out and meet people,' the psychiatrist had said.

George was engaged to be married, so he didn't go. Justin went with Tom. A showband the size of a football team, dressed as Red Indians, waving tomahawks, filled the stage. As soon as the music began, Tom walked straight across to a girl. Justin watched him dancing and talking seriously, took courage and set off across the floor. He recognized a girl who worked in the school kitchen, but she ran into the toilet when he approached. Desperate, he turned to another girl. As they danced he asked where she came from. She said coolly that it was a mile and a half outside the town, and questioned him. When she heard he was a teacher, she told him she was a nurse in the mental hospital, and when he made a date with her she agreed.

Next Monday evening he waited outside the cinema, but she didn't appear, and he drove his aunt's duck-egg blue Renault back to the school. George had made friends already in the local Baptist church, and was at a prayer meeting. Tom was at a teachers' union meeting. The staff room was empty except for Mr Porter, whose false teeth opened in a smile. 'You weren't long.'

'I think I was stood up. Did that ever happen to you?'

'I'm sure it did.' As if cheered by another's failure, Mr Porter talked of his shyness as a young man, of drinking to get courage before a dance. He put a log on the fire and went on talking. One night he had been solicited by a prostitute, he had offered her half a crown, and she had said, 'That'll only get you a sniff of my drawers.' He smiled and looked at Justin until he smiled too. But then, in a voice that made Justin's skin crawl, he asked suddenly, 'Do you think you're better than me?'

'No. Why would I?' Justin said, but as he looked at Mr Porter's white-stubbled chin rippled by red veins, at his cheap suit worn to a black shine, he realized that he did think he was better, and felt horror at the thought of ending up like him.

ONE SATURDAY AFTERNOON the steward drove cattle from a field, the boys put on their togs and played rugby. Most of them didn't know how, but accepted that it was the game they should play because they were Protestant boys. Justin didn't know any Protestant schools, and so he arranged a match with the school where he had been as a boy. The headmaster frowned but gave permission, and a few weeks later Justin set off to Dublin in the school van. His own old rector looked at the raw-boned boys, their cropped hair, their shorts stained green with cow dung, and he murmured, 'They don't exactly smack of the Ascendancy.' They were the poor descendants of camp followers, used to obeying orders, to being called by their surnames. They wolfed the sliced oranges at half-time, and wallowed in the hot shower cubicles afterwards. They muttered replies to the confident, polite suburban boys, stared at the Jesuits' long-winged gowns, the crucifixes on the walls. As Justin drove the rattling blue van back to the country, their voices rose and they talked of all they had seen.

'Well, they were the nicest lads, sir.'

'Are they monks, sir?'

Even when he turned out their dormitory light they went on talking. Their wonder lit up his own past and he saw it from outside, as a world as small as theirs.

SLOWLY HE FELL into their routine. On Sunday afternoons they put on their gaberdine coats and caps and lined up for a walk. As he walked the back roads with them he learned their old-fashioned Christian names and heard their stories of home. Farr became Edwin, who talked of a box of apples his grandmother had sent him. Judd became Cedric, who talked of his foster father, an old clergyman. They talked of other clergymen, the food at Harvest Thanksgivings, their sisters, the crops and livestock in the fields.

When he turned out the light in their dormitory, they called, 'Good night, sir.'

Their loneliness became his own. One night it drove him into town, to the dance hall again, where he met a girl who remained beside him after each set. When he offered to drive her home, she agreed. As soon as they were in his aunt's car she turned to face him, and they kissed. It was the first time he had kissed a girl and not then been pushed politely away. When he did no more than kiss her, she sat back and talked. She worked in County Clare, she was home only for the weekend. When he left her at her door she said she was returning to Clare the next day. But he sang out loud as he drove back to the school.

SOON LETTIE THE MAID was chatting with him as she cleaned his room. He walked the fields with Roy, the steward, searching for a flat place to play cricket when summer came. George's fiancée, Joy, a big young woman in a knitted brown dress, came to visit, bringing a bottle of elderberry wine, which they shared in the staff room, a glass each, when Mr Porter wasn't there. Tom began a debating society, where on Saturday nights the boys argued uneasily, as if they were being set against each other. Justin understood their fear, and as he did his own clouds cleared and the Pole star shone through again. Why tire his neck looking up for that balloon? He was in this small place, beginning a life of his own. He began to write letters to his old friends in Dublin, describing it all.

ONE SUNDAY his parents came down to visit, and he showed them around the school. His father looked at the broad rich fields and shook his head in wonder. 'We were only crofters,' he said. They were country people who had prospered in the city, but never been at ease with their wealth. They were private people, upset by intrusion. They were silent as the headmaster's wife placed them socially and was able to patronize them. As his father shifted from foot to foot like a shy boy, Justin realized that homesick was a poor word for what he had felt in his year abroad; amputated was more accurate. When they were alone again, his mother asked where the Catholic church was, and suddenly angry he told her that he no longer went to Mass. She began to cry. His father's face went grey; he turned aside and whispered hoarsely, 'Why did you have to tell her?' His mother was still crying when she left. But as he stood on the gravel and watched them drive away, he felt relieved. Then the lost feeling returned. His old home was no longer his home. This school was all he had now. When the summer term came and the headmaster asked if he would return in the autumn, he said a helpless Yes.

WHEN HE HEARD that he would be paid every month of the holidays, he decided to go to France, to improve his French. The shock of being alone abroad was still there, but when he saw an Irish nun smile helplessly on the platform at Calais, then scowl as the porter walked past, he was driven to new courage. He took a train to a seaport and found lodgings by the harbour. He bought a thick English novel, *Sinister Street*, which he rationed to fifty pages a day; then he walked the town. When he visited an old prison and found an Irish name carved on the floorboards, he was encouraged again; walking the beach and looking at beautiful distant girls until it was time to go to the restaurant, the big event of his day. As the waitress served his meal one evening her bare shoulder brushed his hair, and she said, '*Pardon*.'

New extremes of loneliness passed over and turned into new confidence. On his way back he spent a night in Paris, where he was so proud of his achievement that the pavements felt like springy grass. In the Gare du Nord, waiting for the boat train, he met someone he knew from home, and the few words they exchanged brought him down to earth, which made him realize that this was his world too, if he wanted it, if he was able for it – and he was!

IT MADE THE SCHOOL and countryside around seem less confining. When he gave Lettie his French cigarettes, which he didn't like, she sat on his bed and smoked one as they talked. When he went down to the pub in the evening, the countrymen remembered his name. The only other countryside he had known was the poor west of Ireland, which his parents had left, where everyone had equally small holdings. It was different here. There were farm labourers without any land, small farmers with twenty or thirty acres, strong farmers who kept hunting horses, and gentry who had somehow held onto most of their estates. It was a stratified society, as cut and sliced as the bog by class and religion.

From the pub he knew the Catholics, and from Sunday church with the boys he knew the Protestants. The Troubles had begun in Northern Ireland, and now he was pressed to take sides. When Mike Reilly got drunk one night and shouted that Bill Galloway was a bloody Orangeman and should be burned out, Justin nodded, shook his head and said, 'Who?' It felt easier when Colonel Browne, the very fat, old man who sat in the front bench of the church, asked him to tea one afternoon. As he walked up a long avenue to a mansion looking over a lake, he felt a glow of snobbish pleasure, but of adventure too: his small safe world was widening. When he recognized the woman who carried the tea tray into the drawing room, he smiled and said, 'Hello, Rose.'

Colonel Browne laughed and said, ' I'd no idea you were on such terms!' Mrs Browne stroked a Siamese cat on her lap and talked of the local people. The girls threw their illegitimate babies into the lake, she said: that was why they never drank the lake water. Colonel Browne talked of a local man who had been their butler, who after a row one day had said he could make life very unpleasant for them. That led straight to politics. When Colonel Browne spoke of IRA assassins, Justin sweated as he tried to explain why the Troubles were inevitable. He was afraid they would throw him out of that big safe house, but Mrs Browne just reached for her cup of China tea – her sun-tanned chest wrinkling like the lake when the wind blew over it; and Colonel Browne just smiled, showing the shining silver fillings in his teeth – and listened, which made Justin talk more. Despite himself, he was growing up.

One night he walked home from the pub with Mike Reilly, and as they drank whiskey from teacups in a ruined kitchen he learned that Mike's wife had gone. Mike pointed to a faded newspaper photo pinned to the wall, of himself as a long-legged, handsome young jockey winning a race. That was all he remembered, though they talked until almost dawn; and though he was drunk he made his way back to the school over fields white with frost and moonlight. He was finding his feet.

JANE, one of his old university friends, answered his letter with an invitation to a party. The embossed card said At Home. He had been away for so long that he felt like the schoolboys as he drove up to the city, and through the suburban roads where he had been reared. He didn't call to his parents: he was starting a new life of his own. Jane told the others what an amusing life he led, but when he didn't amuse them, they went back to talking among themselves. Most of them were lawyers, they all wore suits; he counted five sets of cuff links as he stood alone. Jane introduced him to a shy fat girl with goose-pimpled legs, then joined the others' conversation. The girl looked at him in silence, as if at her reflection in a mirror.

Then he walked over to Jane and said, 'I have to drive back to the country. I'd better go.'

'Of course. I understand.' As she saw him to the door, she squeezed his arm and said, 'Keep in touch.'

He squeezed her arm and said, 'We must go out together some night.'

'Of course.' She shook his hand firmly, to make things clear.

It made something clear. As he drove back to the school, he said suddenly aloud, 'Jesus Christ, never again.'

THE OTHER SIDE of his old life had been in the west, where as a boy he had spent holidays. Now, when an uncle died suddenly, he drove there to the funeral. After a year in his new home this countryside of memories seemed threadbare. He had half-forgotten the flattened tar-barrels and old bedframes used as gates, the poor small fields, the friendly Lancashire accents of the women who had married local emigrants. His uncle had been one of those emigrants, but had never married; nor had his aunt. She cried and put her arms about him and asked why had God taken her brother? She had asked for so little, she said: someone to watch TV with in the evenings, to have sitting across the hearth. But as he watched TV with her in the evenings, as she sat the teapot on his Penguin book, talked of her sister's drinking, took the tongs irritably to rearrange the fire he had laid, his anger returned. It was from that cramped home as much as from his Dublin one that he had fled abroad, and failed. He was glad to return to the middle ground he had found for himself, where he could start again, alone.

AS ANOTHER spring came he went for walks along the back roads, exploring. One day at a signpost he met an old man on a bicycle, with a bundle on the back-carrier, who asked him the way to Ballinasloe. Justin showed him down to the main road. It stayed with him all night. Sitting at the head of the big classroom, supervising the boys' study, he pictured the old man pushing through the dark to that country his mother had come from; and for a wonderful few hours he understood, and felt freed from her fierce nostalgia. Slowly, he was waking up.

The headmaster had his own nostalgia for an imagined world, and as spring turned into summer he spoke of cricket again. He showed Justin a few stumps and a cracked bat in a tea chest, then directed him to Bill Galloway who might have something more. Following another back road, Justin found that it became the avenue to a big house. Wind was blowing through old beech trees; wood pigeons with puffed-out pink breast feathers looked down at him with small bright black eyes. It was a place where he would have expected to find another Anglo-Irish gentleman, but Bill Galloway was plain.

He had been to the school where Justin was teaching, and his accent was as local as Mike Reilly's, though with a firm tone. He said he played some local cricket and would gladly lend his equipment when the school had a proper field. He was up in his tractor, setting out to plough, but he sat there chatting of his life. His father had been born on a farm in England, but a remote relation had left him this Irish farm. Not sure what to do, he and his workman had cycled to Liverpool every Friday evening, taken the boat to Dublin and cycled down to maintain this place; then on Monday returned to England for another week. In the end, Bill said, his father had settled in this better, Irish place. Justin asked if he had ever seen the English farm. Bill shook his head and said that he had never been to England.

A man crossed the yard to join them. Justin remarked on his voice, and he said that he had come from Mayo to work there twenty years ago. When he had gone, Bill said that he had come with only the clothes he stood up in and a kettle. The random way each had settled there, the way Bill spoke of the west of Ireland in the same easy incurious voice he spoke of England made this small safe place seem open to the wide world. Justin's walks took him further week by week.

Bob was another of the Protestant neighbours, a tall, lean, serious man with black curly hair, silver-streaked. He wore an old long coat of brown herringbone tweed to church on Sunday, and afterwards crossed the road to the pub for a single glass of whiskey. Bachelors tend to be very tidy or very untidy. Bob was very tidy. He was whitewashing the gateway to his farm when Justin wandered by one day. Bob finished a slow brushstroke, set the brush across the pail, then stood to talk. His brown hands were spotless. His great-grandfather had come from Yorkshire, he said, and arrived in this place only because it was as far as the fare allowed. The coach had set him down; he had found a bed for the night, and soon after found a job as what Bob called an 'usher' in the school where Justin taught. He had married, and in time his son had bought a few dozen acres, which Bob inherited. Justin learned that Bob had no time for parsons, or Anglo-Irish landowners; that he had refused Colonel Browne permission to shoot over his land, and refused the hunt, too. Then Bob picked up his brush and went back to whitewashing his gateway.

EACH OF THOSE meetings gave Justin a root in that small place, and he felt himself growing with its nourishment. He was always hungry at dinnertime, and so tired after the day's work that he slept without pills. One Sunday afternoon a pack of beagles met at the crossroads, and he recognized the master as a man he had seen working in the National Library in a khaki coat. Seeing him here in a green velvet coat, up to his knees in wet rushes, drew the city from the smothering past into Justin's own present experience, and another root went down into that land. His aunt who drank phoned late one night, to ask what he had been saying about her to his other aunt; she cried, then asked for her car back, and put down the phone. His other aunt wrote to say her sister was drinking again, and asked him to visit soon. He said that he couldn't, as he had no car. He was relieved. Now he was alone in this middle place with his new friends.

MIKE REILLY saddled an old hunter, showed him how his legs should grip and the stirrups take his weight, so he balanced on the rhythm of the horse. As another summer came he rode in the evenings up and down Mike's sloping fields, walled by wild hawthorn on the hilltop and at the bottom by a double ditch, a dyke of deep water between huge earthen banks where old trees grew. Walking to Mike's stable one evening, he stopped at the main road and – as anxious, as eager as if he were jumping the dyke – thumbed a lift into town, where he stood at the canal bridge until another car pulled alongside.

The man chatted about local news and asked what the lads were up to, all so casually that it was a while before Justin realized he was being pumped for information about the IRA. Seeing that he knew nothing, the man said he was on his way to a night's duty in Dublin, that he was a guard in the Special Branch. He spent the journey talking of his hard upbringing, of his days in the army, of masturbating competitions that the soldiers held at night, with sixpence as a prize. He left Justin at the arch of Christ Church Cathedral, and said he would be there again at midnight on his way back.

Now that he no longer visited his parents or old friends each time he went there, the city didn't seem his smothering home. He walked the crowded streets, stood and looked up at pigeons roosting in the Bank of Ireland portico, like any other stranger. He saw a gallery where an exhibition was opening, and when he went inside and someone talked to him, he felt the same excitement he'd had in the Paris railway station when he met an old friend. All this was his, if he wanted it. Afterwards the stranger asked him to a party, in a flat on the quays. The windows looked over the black shining river; there was a scent of dope smoke in the tall old rooms. Someone sat on the floor with a block of Chinese ink, brushing letters on a sheet of paper; some people were dancing, the song of the year was playing on a gramophone:

'If her daddy's rich, take her out for a meal,
If her daddy's poor, just do what you feel.'

He didn't know what he felt except anxiety, and that it was better than Jane's party. The Christ Church bells were striking midnight as he crossed the river, and a few minutes later the guard stopped under the arch. Now they hadn't so much talk. The guard asked about his evening, but when Justin told him of the art exhibition and the party, he was silent. When Justin asked him about his night's duty, he didn't reply. His heavy face stared at the road ahead, he drove at sixty on the straight stretch by the canal. When they came to the town, he stopped in the main street and said slowly, 'Will you walk the rest?' His face had a dark smile as Justin hesitated, a scowl as he got out. It was three in the morning when he reached the school, but he felt so frightened and elated that he sat up playing records on Mr Porter's old gramophone in the staff room until dawn.

AS NATURALLY as he had come to learn the boys' names, now he knew the people in the cottages and farmhouses that had seemed so strange a year before. When he saw wild birds flock above the road he knew that Rose was out walking, throwing stale bread along the verge. Colonel Browne stopped his van whenever he saw him, and rolled down his window to talk. In the pub at closing time he was invited into the kitchen to drink whiskey with the old parish priest. He learned that the woman Rose lived with was her illegitimate daughter, that Colonel Browne's wife suffered from her nerves. He was settling deeper in this place. One autumn evening the headmaster took him to a Harvest Thanksgiving in a tiny church, filled with the scent of vegetables and fruit and ripe wheat sheaves, where an old man with a white moustache scraped the hymn music on a violin. Driving home through blowing drifts of golden beech leaves, the headmaster gave a fatherly smile and said, 'I always wanted to be able to share all this with someone.' Justin didn't return the smile. Suddenly he wanted to be able to share all this with someone else.

GEORGE MARRIED JOY and moved to a cottage in the school grounds, where they invited him one evening to meet their pastor. But when they knelt down after tea – under a poker-work plaque that said, 'Cooking lasts, kissing don't!' – and prayed for Justin's salvation, he felt that it was a place where he would not be easy again.

Tom too was finding his own way. He asked Justin to go with him to a Fianna Fáil rally in the town, where a minister spoke to the crowd from a platform. When Tom heckled with a question, a woman struck them both on the shoulders with an umbrella, the minister looked down with studied sadness and asked was this what Ireland had come to? The crowd shouted, 'Communists!' A guard escorted them to the end of the Main Street, and told them not to return. Tom was excited, talking of his father, who had been in the Communist Party, as they walked the long road back to the school. Justin felt he was listening to Mr Porter calling Latin verbs from the classroom. He understood, but it meant nothing to him.

Even Mr Porter left the school one Friday evening to visit Dublin. When he came back on Sunday night he was so drunk that he couldn't teach for the rest of the week. The smell from his bedroom, of old flesh sweating out whiskey and nicotine, carried into the corridor; each time Justin passed it, his dread of wasting his life there returned.

AGAIN THE DAYS grew short, but he borrowed Mike Reilly's old hunter more often in the evenings, galloping up and down the same few fields until he sweated like the horse. From there he could see across the silent countryside to the lake. He was twenty-four; next year he would be twenty-five. He took to riding along the back roads, and one day found a stables where there was more land to gallop on, the demesne of an almost derelict mansion, which Bernie, a local woman, now owned. She was small, fat and handsome, lame from a fall, always in old riding breeches so torn that strips of the yellow leather lining flapped between her legs as she walked. When she saw that he could ride well enough not to be in danger, she left him alone.

As soon as he mounted, the horse ran alongside a wall so closely that his arm was scraped raw. Next, the horse galloped under low branches of a tree, but he was in the saddles still. Finally the horse walked into a pond and stood there, belly-deep. The water was mirror-calm again when another horse appeared, going back to the yard. Justin's horse followed. That was how he met Geraldine.

She had a slight limp, he noticed when she dismounted. They

talked as they unsaddled and rubbed their horses down. She lived in the town; she came out once a week to learn how to ride. Then they each paid Bernie their ten shillings and said goodbye.

Two years of work and meals and sleep had calmed him. The school had become a big family, with the same gossip, laughter, aspirations and rows. The headmaster asked sixth-form boys to breakfast, as if he were a university tutor and they were the gilded youth who would run the country one day. When a boy pocketed the silver teaspoons and sold them in the town, a dark thrill ran through the school. When Lettie the maid inherited a fortune from a distant cousin, the whole school – even Mr Porter – rejoiced, and was sad when she had gone. Justin realized how happy he was in this small place, and wanted more than ever to share it with someone else.

WHEN HE RETURNED next week to the riding school, Geraldine was there. They rode out together under the stable-yard arch and down the avenue. Again the chestnut leaves were darkening, the light-green chestnut shells had filled. When her horse shied at a blown piece of paper they slowed to a walk, talking as the road led them around the big lake and up the slopes on the other side. She said her father was a bank manager; she had grown up in a dozen market towns. He said that explained her accent, which seemed to belong to no particular place. She asked where he lived, and he said he taught in the Protestant school. She described one of the schools she had been to, with small glass booths like telephone boxes in which they had practised the violin. He asked was her father in the Bank of Ireland, she said he was, and Justin said they had met. The road went over the slopes and down into flat land that turned to bog. When they came to a long stony shallow lake, as jagged-pointed at either end as the Neolithic flint knife he had found, they dismounted, and explored a ruined house. She had heard that a nobleman had ended his days there. He had heard from Colonel Browne that the nobleman had been disgraced. It was almost dark as they rode back along the bog road, so they trotted again, then cantered, and as the horses neared home they galloped hard. She was as flushed and excited as he when they arrived. While they unsaddled and rubbed their horses down, he asked would she like to go out with him some night. She agreed. As she looked up at him and the stable's cobwebbed light bulb showed her smile, he kissed her suddenly. Then he hurried away to the ramshackle house to give his ten shillings to Bernie.

HE WAS ANXIOUS now, but was restless in the school. When the local rector invited George and Joy, Tom and him to dinner in the glebe house, he was glad to go out. The clergyman was lame – so many people there were lame – and minded like a child by his wife. They had an adopted son, who had grown up, gone away and never returned – the schoolboys said – so they couldn't mention that. They sat at a small oval table in a dining room painted dark green, talking about the school and looking out the window at a big yew tree when a silence fell. When dinner was over the rector's wife said to Joy, 'We'll leave the men to talk.' They stood as the two women left the room, then the rector took a bottle of Sandeman port from the sideboard and they sat down. The yew tree faded into darkness as the rector told stories of his own school. He asked them a question that a master had asked him in Scripture class: 'What did Saint Paul find when he went into the desert?' George stared out at the dark, as if searching the Scriptures, frowned and gave up. Then the rector gave his old master's answer: 'He found no water.' George's bewildered face made Justin laugh, which turned out to be in order, for the rector explained that it was a joke, which made Justin laugh more, and then he was out of control, whimpering like one of the boys in class until he had to leave the room. As they went back to the school, Tom said, 'What a limited life,' and Justin thought again of his coming test.

WHEN HE WENT to the riding school on his next half-day, Geraldine wasn't there. He rode for an hour about the ruined park, testing his courage by jumping the trunk of a fallen tree, then returned to the yard. As he dismounted, she appeared from a stable, leading her horse, and he asked suddenly would she like to go out with him next Saturday? She said she would, then she rode out under the arch, ducking her head as usual, though the arch was twelve feet high.

The staff room was empty on Saturday evening, except for old Mr Porter, who looked at Justin's new black cord jacket, grey trousers, polished black shoes, white shirt and dark blue tie, then his teeth shifted into a smile. 'You're all dressed up.'

'I asked a girl out to dinner.'

'Good lad. Where are you going to take her?'

'There's a new restaurant. It's called The Road House.'

'How'll you get there?'

'George is lending me his car.'

'That was nice of him,' Mr Porter said, and his teeth made another smile.

The lonely boys gathered, clapping his back as he crossed the high-walled yard, waving as he drove down the avenue and rattled over the cattle grid. When he called to the bank house, Geraldine's mother led him upstairs to their rooms. She was tall and thin with a stiff anxious look, as if someone had a finger in her back. Her husband gave Justin a drink, had another himself and talked about golf. A sister of Geraldine's, pretty but sharp-faced, talked to him about Dublin. Then Geraldine appeared, looking so beautiful that he became afraid, and then he was alone with her in George's car driving to The Road House, wondering what they could talk about.

He couldn't ask what she did, in case she did nothing, which might have something to do with her limp. He couldn't talk about his year abroad, in case that led to explaining why he had returned. They were silent as they sat at a window table with a view of the new main road. Her fair hair was brushed shining; her pale cheeks were as bright. She wore a dress open at the collar, showing the slightest parting of white breasts. He looked over her shoulder at the speeding cars, half-wishing he was in one of them; but all that was of his own making was here, scattered in the countryside he could see beyond the road, where he had begun to live again.

He asked for wine and drank a glass, then talked about the school: how the boys were often hungry and stole potatoes to cook in the fields; how Mr Porter had come back from the city one night so drunk that he couldn't walk up the avenue, until George had taken his arm and said that another man had climbed a hill once, though he had fallen three times.

Geraldine said that she didn't like wine. She blushed and said that she liked music, but knew only the elements; she and her mother belonged to the local music society. Last summer they had sung in Wicklow, where they had found beautiful shells scattered along the shore. But between each run of conversation he heard their silence, as loud as the conversation from the tables all around. He drank so much wine that he had to excuse himself. The two doors were marked Him and Hers. When he got back to the table, she had finished eating. It was so early when they got back to the town that he suggested they go for a walk.

Sam Hutchinson, who worked in the big drapery shop and came out to the school every Sunday to play the harmonium at

Evensong, said Hello to him. A woman smiled and said Hello to her. They walked up the long main street, stopping to look in each shop window. In the windows' reflection he saw in her face the same imploring wish to talk as in his own. They walked as far as the canal bridge and looked down at the still water. She said that her father had said this was the exact centre of the country, what was called the Spine, so the water flowed from there both to the east and west. He couldn't think of any reply. It was dark when they walked back down the main street, so they couldn't see the shop windows, and couldn't be seen. As they approached the bank they stood into the stationery shop doorway between two bay windows covered with amber cellophane, and they kissed goodbye. Somehow her tongue met his and then they put their arms around each other, swaying forwards and back.

HE DIDN'T KNOW what to do next, and now he noticed his new loneliness. It was worst on Sundays, when the Protestants went home after church. The Catholics went to the pub after Mass, then home to dinner and then to a Gaelic football match. Their crowded cars roared down the small roads, and there was silence again. When he went to the pub it was empty except for the landlord, sitting on a bench with Mike Reilly's daughter, a girl of fifteen. When Justin noticed that they were holding hands, he looked away. But it encouraged him. Then an excuse to do nothing came: there was a teachers' strike. In his firm way Tom explained the union's demands to the headmaster. The headmaster closed the school.

Justin went back to the city, to sleep in his old bedroom, and after one night it seemed as if he had never left. His mother still wrote weekly letters to his aunt in the country, and still dreaded that she might come to stay. His father listened on the phone to his sister who drank until his face was grey. His brothers went to the end of the garden and talked business as they drove golf balls into a net. His aunt came up for a week from the country; his mother withdrew to the kitchen and cooked big meals. When his aunt went into the kitchen to help, there were disagreements that became fantastic rows. One evening when the doorbell rang and his aunt tried to answer. His mother stopped her, and when his aunt insisted, his mother stood between her and the door. Looking at them locked in silent wrestling, he saw the confusion of courage and kindness, pettiness and timidity in which he had been reared. There was something in that tangle he loved and hated and needed, that imprisoned him still. When Tom phoned a few days later and said he was going to London until the strike was over, Justin was eager to go too.

THEY ARGUED about the strike on the mail boat, although he wasn't interested. He had learned by now that he wasn't cut out to teach. At Holyhead there was a hammering of shoes on the platform as young countrymen ran to the news stall to buy *Penthouse* and *Playboy* magazines. As Tom looked at them with pity, Justin saw that one reason he wasn't a good teacher was that he had no interest in keeping discipline. As the train crossed Anglesey, Welsh navvies raised their shovels and called, 'Good morning, Patrick!' Tom didn't smile. But Justin was glad of his orderly company. When they reached Euston, Tom went to the news stall and bought a paper. In a few hours they had found a room.

Next day they found jobs in hotel kitchens – Tom in The Dorchester and Justin in the Park Lane. In the evening the fog was so thick that he crossed Hyde Park step by step, both hands held before him, feeling his way into the great city. Again, everything was new and strange. One night in the Underground two smooth-faced young men were talking to each other in loud voices. Two rough-faced young men muttered remarks:

'Couple of pouffs.'

'Yeah, queering about.'

One of the smooth-faced young men laid his umbrella on the platform, took off his bowler hat and black jacket, opened his cuff-links and rolled up his white sleeves. But then the other one cried, 'No, I say, Peter, don't!' Justin felt his disappointment. He was longing for some showdown that would set him free.

He stood at a sink all day washing dishes with a Pakistani boy named Shakir. They wore long aprons, but their shoes were always wet. None of the waiters and waitresses talked to Shakir, he noticed, but a couple talked to him.

'No cure for that sickness,' Beryl said when the still-room girl got sick one morning.

'Why's that?' he said.

Beryl looked at him. 'You Irish then?'

'Don't sound Irish.' Cecil chewed his pork pie. 'You sound educated-like.'

When he told them about the teachers' strike, Beryl looked at him again. 'Go on,' she said. 'You got a degree and all?'

'Course it's easier in Ireland,' Cecil said.

Cecil had been a waiter since the War. He carried a weight of low wisdom as big as his belly. 'There's a nice fuck,' he murmured, turning his thumb towards Shakir.

Justin was shocked. Everything in London seemed sinful, from Cecil's yellow face to Beryl's peroxide hair. His voice sounded plaintive against the definite English one. London seemed like a machine that would crush anything not adapted to its movements. But as he sat on a park bench one long Sunday afternoon and an old man sat down beside him, read a Greek newspaper from front page to back and then went away, all with an easy silence, the freedom of this life shone out like the Pole star. Again the great thought returned: all this was his, if he wanted it. Another day, in Charing Cross, he stepped into a small bookshop, where a man in a bowler hat and dark coat was looking gravely through a tray of black and white photographs. Justin glimpsed one, of a naked girl with wire tied tightly about her breasts, and he hurried outside – where another man in a bowler hat and dark coat asked him directions, which he was able to give! He went suddenly into another shop, bought a card and posted it to Geraldine.

He didn't mention her to Tom. They got on well together but hardly talked. It was only when the strike had ended and they were on the train to Holyhead, that Tom said he was leaving the school, and returning to university next year to study politics. Justin realized that their ways had parted, as smoothly as the points clicked on the railway.

JOY HAD a baby now, and when classes ended George went to their cottage in the grounds. Tom went to study in his room. Mr Porter, his false teeth open, his yellow tongue hanging out, slept in an armchair by the fire. When payday came, Justin was glad to escape into the town.

'We haven't seen you for a long time.' Geraldine's father reached through the thin brass rails and shook his hand.

'I was away.'

'We heard that. We heard that.'

'How is Geraldine?'

'You'll have to ask her that yourself.' Her father smiled, stamped the back of the cheque, and said, 'Why don't you call one evening, visit us at home?'

He said, 'Thank you,' but he didn't go. His life had been a running away from home. He had found a home here, a hiding place where he could find himself. He didn't go to the bank again, he didn't go to the riding school, and yet he longed to see Geraldine. He couldn't understand it.

'Still wandering?' the rector's wife said when she met him on the road. 'You're still looking for your other half.'

He walked the back roads every evening, talking with Colonel Browne and Mike Reilly, with Bob and Rose, and Bill Galloway. Bill especially stood for all that he liked in this small place. Bill bought his newspaper in the pub, wasn't afraid of Colonel Browne, gave Mike Reilly's daughter work as a babysitter, and when it was raining he gave Rose a lift. In the same way, when the headmaster had finally asked his help in making a cricket pitch, Bill had agreed. By the time Justin returned from England, a field behind the farmyard had become a brilliant green.

On Saturday evenings Bill came to level it with the long iron roller he drew across his spring wheat, washed his hands until they were as red as the school's carbolic soap, then went home. On Sundays he went to church with his family, morning and evening. On Mondays he began work again. Everything was slow and orderly. One evening he had the schoolboys pull an old garden roller, a solid drum of limestone, up and down the wicket until it was smooth and tight. Afterwards, excited by their freedom, the boys pushed the roller so hard that it ran off the field and down a slope where it shattered against the high wall. Bill's face clouded – the only time Justin had seen him upset – and then it was clear again.

In a few weeks spring opened into summer. The fields disappeared behind growing walls of green; then hawthorn and elderflowers made the hedges white. When Rose walked the road, a smaller flock of birds circled overhead. As naturally, the cricket season began. Bill helped Justin to arrange a match – the school team against a county one – and as the players in their old whites stood in place about the pitch, it looked as if it had been there forever, like the old trees standing in their pools of shade.

Justin was playing with the boys on the school team. The head-master agreed gladly to play on the other side – for Bill had rounded up some old county gentlemen as well as ordinary folk. His wife supervised the tea. There was almost a crowd standing about the boundary. Colonel Browne and his wife sat on school chairs. Bob stood alone in his long brown tweed overcoat. Even Mike Reilly was there, looking uneasily about. His daughter and another girl left their bikes in the ditch outside the school gates and walked tiptoe up the avenue, as if into another land. The headmaster was in his element, talking to an old man with an Oxford accent and huge purple hands. He wore his old Trinity blazer, even as he went out to bat. A silence came over the field, and the match began.

Justin opened the bowling, and by a terrible fluke hit the stumps with his first ball. The silence remained for a moment, like a shot bird before it falls. Then the boys cheered suddenly, savagely, and – with a hurt, puzzled look at Justin – the headmaster walked away. The rest of the innings was a blur. It wasn't until teatime that he saw Geraldine and her mother were there.

He went cold with fright and hot with excitement as he approached them. Bill's wife introduced them as friends from the music society. Geraldine's mother said that they had met already, and Bill's wife left them alone.

'I was away.' He blushed. 'Did you get my postcard?'

'I did.' She smiled and looked at his face, and then her mother moved away.

It was wonderful to find her in that small place. He told her about his job in London, and described the Park Lane Hotel. She laughed as he told her how he had gone there for tea one after-noon, and what the manager had said when he found out. He told her of going to a fish and chip shop in Piccadilly one night, where an elegant man called, 'Barrow in Furnace, Nineteen-Forty-Five?' and a small man frying the chips looked up at him, then winked and said, 'That's right!'

Bill came by and said to her, 'Don't listen to that fella!' His wife called them up to tea.

'Would you like to join me?' Geraldine smiled and looked at his face again.

He went on talking as they stood at the long trestle table. He could hear himself, as if he had a finger in one ear. It was as if all the energy of the past three years was being released. He told her how Mr Porter had been sacked. He described his many aunts. She began to talk of the local music society. He interrupted, asking if she still played the violin.

She smiled and said, 'Sorry?'

'Didn't you learn it at school? In a glass box!' He laughed, and talked again.

She smiled again, but not so much, and when more people came up for tea she stepped back quietly from the table. Her face changed and she said, 'Thank you.'

'You've had enough?' he said.

She walked away. He hurried after her. 'What did I say?'

'Nothing.' Her blushing embarrassment gave her voice a power that turned him cold.

'What's wrong?'

'Nothing. I asked you to have tea with me.' She said, 'Thank you,' again, then crossed the field and stood talking with her mother.

He stood, trying to remember what he had said, but all he could remember was her trembling 'Nothing.' It meant that his talk had held her at arm's length, that he was afraid of being caught, that he didn't take this place to heart, that it had been a place to rest in, and that he was better now. But he couldn't grasp that. When he looked again she had gone. The players went back onto the field and stood in the lengthening shadows of the trees. This was where his three years in the country had led him. He knew then he would leave.

THERE WAS a shout from the wicket — one of the stumps was down. Bill was fielding on the boundary, bent forward, hands on thighs. He straightened slowly when the umpire raised his finger. Justin went over to the rope.

'Bill?'

'I was thinking it was you.' The same slow Westmeath accent. 'I saw you there and I said to myself, that's Justin Kelly.'

'How are you?' He looked at the thin grey hair, the glasses so unlikely on his out-of-doors face.

'Still playing. We have our own team now.' The same reserved smile. 'That was my son bowling. I'd better go over to him.' Bill turned away and ran slowly across the field.

It had been too small. He had been too young. He had hardly known her. It could never have worked out. He had been hiding from life. He would have died of boredom, drunk like Mr Porter. There had been many more years of travelling before he grew up enough to settle down. He could never have knitted the tangled sides of his life together if he had stayed ... But seeing Bill run slowly back to a tall skinny young man in his twenties and embrace him, he felt a small stupid disappointment, as if he had arrived at a station just as the train pulled out.

The Lower Deck

WE STOOD on the pavement as the coffin was taken from the house. It's a time when you speak to those neighbours you usually just nod to. Mr Gray said, 'What's it all about at all?' Miss Byrne said, 'She knows now. She's saying to herself – So that's what it is.' It's a time when you realize that the past, which seemed so solid, was no different from this; that this is your home now, and these people will come to your funeral. We walked behind the hearse down to the church. Someone said, 'It's like Belfast.' A dog trotted alongside. Afterwards I went for a drink with Alex. He didn't want to go back to the house alone.

A young woman came in, wearing a 1920s' cloche hat, pink and black, flattened like a beret; black eyeshadow; a black thin sweater showing low, heavy breasts; black stockings and boots; about 5′ 8″. She was followed by a young man, about 3′ 8″, so small that he climbed onto the bar stool rung by rung. Sitting, they were equal. Eating crisps, he dropped one, climbed down and came up with it in his mouth. She looked about coldly, rolling a cigarette, and saw me stare — for a moment I thought she was going to come over and slap my face. After one drink they left. The barman said, 'She's only going out with him for show.'

The new bar girl — low-cut dress, intelligent face — was gazing out the window at the dark. The barman went over to the window and joined her. As he went back behind the counter he said, 'A taxi driver riding the arse off a girl in his car.'

Someone said, 'The landscape's changed since our day.'

A lot has changed since I came here as a boy. It seemed a shabby, out-of-the-way place then, where no one would find me as I savoured bitter Guinness, a Bristol cigarette and the newspaper list of banned books. We were so oppressed then, we didn't know we were oppressed. The titles were like gifts from a munificent ruler: *Sins of Cynthia* ... *Velvet-Tongued Suzi* ... *Nurse's Weakness* ... *Wicked Work*. Even when I came here to live, this pub was the same: bare walls and partitions, lino on the floor. I was in the bar the night the news of John Lennon's murder came through. The car park was still a harbour then.

I wanted to say to Alex, 'I slept with her once.' It would draw a circle around everything. But you can't say that.

SHE WAS COMING ALONG the canal bank. I hadn't seen her for years. Her hair was dyed brown, she had some crazy brown lipstick on. She looked terrible. 'Triona,' I said, 'how are you?'

She said, 'I'm fucking separated.' She took a big scissors from her handbag, stooped and snipped at the grass. Her laugh was too loud.

'Would you like a drink?' She noticed my wedding ring. 'Oh God, you're married. '

I was working in the language school. I had stepped out between classes for a breath of air. I said I'd call to see her one evening. She was back home.

We had hardly known each other, but growing up in the same suburban road, walking to Mass, seeing our parents nod to each other had made us part of one family. You heard things somehow. Her father was supposed to go through *The Observer* on Sunday morning with a scissors, cutting out unsuitable bits. We think when we are young that no one notices us, but she had noticed me, as I had noticed her. I remember her sailing over Portobello Bridge on her bike one day, as if going into town for some adventure. 'You looked so serious,' she said afterwards. I was probably going to the Lower Deck, to read the latest list of banned books.

When I called she was in the kitchen, sitting beside the Aga in a small armchair. Her mother asked about my parents, made tea, mouthed the word *depressed*, then left us alone. Triona hardly raised her head. I had never seen anyone bite their knuckles before. I didn't see her again for about a year.

I was at an auction; she was sitting behind. Afterwards I showed her an old painting I had bought, of two boys riding horses into the sea. 'Are you serious?' she said. She had a dry sad tone that was attractive. We chatted as we walked down the road.

She had gone to Barcelona straight after her Leaving. She would have gone anywhere, but she had done Spanish at school. She married some academic there and settled down. Her life passed in a daze of cooking and having sex all over the house. He used to put his hand up her skirt when she was on the phone to her mother. When he ran off with one of his students, she had come home.

'You look better,' I said. She did too. There was sparkle in her eye as she told me she had a new boyfriend. 'Remember Alex?'

Things happen that can twist you. She had flown from home; thinking abroad would be like those parties we all gave when our parents were out. But when no parents came home, she had been left alone with her innocent wildness. It had pulled her in, like a sleeve caught in a machine. All that was part of the nightmare became her definition of what life should be. It had to be — otherwise her flight would have been a failure.

She was living in a redbrick terrace, just a few streets from mine. When I told her that, she said, 'Just like the old days,' and gave another dry smile. She pointed to one of the houses. 'That was a brothel until last week. Twenty quid for a ride. Not bad.' Her eyes had that fixed sparkle again. 'Do you want to come in?'

Of course she had been 'wild', but we all had been, like butter-flies fluttering against a windowpane. The windows were open by the time she came back, but she was stuck fluttering inside. It was sad. The living room was shadowed by an old backyard wall of rubble-brick and stone. She set two mugs on a counter littered with envelopes. 'You look busy,' I said.

She was a dressmaker now, and while the kettle boiled she showed me her workroom, a big bright room upstairs, overlooking the yard. There was a table covered in cloths, pins and scissors. A mannequin was fitted with a silky evening gown. She picked up a ribbon of black velvet and tied it around her throat. She said, 'Alex jumps on me when I wear this.'

She left it on while she made coffee. I looked at old prints and shelves of old books. 'And you're a collector,' I said.

'They belong to Alex.' She raised her eyebrows in a way that made me feel guilty when he came in.

In the way of childhood we had been friends for a short while, walking home together after school. I remembered the shift and crunch of gravel on their front path, the big garden at the back. I had a memory of his mother gathering ripe blue damsons from a tree buzzing with wasps. Now Alex was a heavy-faced, middle-aged man in a pinstripe suit, a red silk handkerchief spilling from the breast pocket. He wore a signet ring, God help him. He lay in an armchair, flopped one leg across the other and drawled, 'I've seen you about.'

'Strange,' I said. 'I never noticed you.'

A soft hurt smile showed through his manner. 'I'm used to that.'

Triona turned to me. 'What flirtatious socks you're wearing.'

Alex looked up. 'Sorry?'

'I wasn't talking to you.'

His voice slipped into something rougher. 'You'll find your head in your lap, if you're not careful.'

She went up to her workroom, but her mocking presence remained. As if defying it, Alex talked of old school friends and what they were doing now, of priests and parents who had died. The books had been his father's. Some of them, wrapped in brown paper, were first editions. He turned on the light and pointed out a rare print on the wall. Triona called down, 'Don't forget to show him the old school photo.'

Stubborn, Alex drawled back, 'I won't.'

She came down only when I was leaving, with pins between her teeth, a scissors in her hand. My heart went out to him. She was back with a man like her father to mind her, whom she could punish now.

Next time we met, she was walking along the canal bank. She had a dog on a leash, a fox terrier – she was doing her best to settle in. A handsome young man in white shirt and tight black trousers went by. 'Yum, yum,' she murmured. 'Who's that?'

'He could be a waiter in the restaurant.'

She laughed. 'That's where I met Alex.'

'There was money there all right.'

'Not any more. He's a waiter.'

'Alex is a waiter?'

'Head waiter, actually.' She did a genteel voice.

'What happened?'

'The usual Irish. Drink.'

That explained a lot: Alex's flushed face and guarded manner, the assertive prosperity, the turning back to the good old days. Passing the restaurant one night, I looked in the picture window and saw him showing people to tables, drawing out the chairs with little flourishes. His pinstripe suit and floppy red handkerchief seemed a big bluff, like the restaurant. It had been a fashionable place once, where businessmen with expense accounts brought clients for showy meals, the chef signed his name in vanilla scribbles along the side of square dessert plates, and a saucer of handmade chocolates took the sting from the rip-off bill. Lately, another smaller restaurant was taking its trade away.

I saw him another night having a smoke outside the kitchen door with an old waiter. His cheeks sucked in as he drew on the cigarette, then he threw it in the gutter and went back inside. One evening I saw him crouched double, looking across a tabletop to see that the knives and forks were aligned. Our eyes met, but he showed no recognition, as if he was ashamed.

'I mean, it's the ideal set-up for an affair,' Triona said. 'He's out every night.' She didn't even disguise her indifference now.

'Do you want that?'

'I think staying with him would be a total cop-out.'

'Alex is nice.'

'Alex is nice. Everyone says that. But he doesn't interest me.'

'Why not find someone who does?'

'I was down in the Clarence the other night, and this country guy asked me up to his room. I said, I suppose you want to fuck me? Do you know, he turned crimson? Nothing has changed here. It's just the same as when I left.'

She was just the same. She smiled to an old man walking a Yorkshire terrier. When he had passed, she said, 'What's the story there? That dog's always on the go.'

It was a joke in the neighbourhood. The old couple clung together but didn't get on. As soon as the husband came in from a walk, his wife set out for another one.

'That'll be me, if I stay with Alex.'

We came to her terrace, and though it was late she asked me in for tea. She didn't turn on the light. When I kept my distance, she turned on the TV. A small tenor was singing some duet with a deep-chested soprano. 'I'd say she'd be the one on top.' Her eyes gave their sparkle. 'What do you think?'

I shrugged but that seemed cold, and as I was leaving I kissed her cheek. She took my hand and placed it on her breast. Her eyes closed. She was like a child alone with a box of sweets. She looked relieved when I drew away.

Alex was right for her. There was something between them: her failed marriage, his comedown in the world; his old rarities; her silk gowns. I could see how they had come together. I wanted their dream to come true.

What had not happened between us made us friends. I was going for the paper one morning when she called me. She wore a black suit and carried a red plastic folder; she was talking with some builders who were gutting an old house. 'Well, lads, I'll leave you to it,' she said in a voice that tried to be like theirs. As we walked down the street I heard her news. She had a job in a property business. Her dressmaking was too much work for too little return. She was settling down, growing up.

'How's the job?' I said, next time we ran into each other.

'OK.'

'It's better,' I said. 'Regular work, regular pay.'

'That. And I'm having an affair with the boss.'

I felt sad, but just said, 'He should be flattered.'

'I don't care if he is or not. I'm doing it for myself. We were in Madrid for the weekend.'

'Does Alex know?'

'He's sleeping downstairs. Pathetic. He dragged the spare bed down the other night.'

I left them to it, glimpsing how things were now and then, as you glimpse bits of a programme in TV shop windows: Triona coming home in the morning, looking dreamy; Alex coming out of the pub, wiping his mouth with the back of his hand, a *Times* clipped under his arm, his polished heavy black shoes crunching the grit. It brought home the struggle that was still going on. Neither would yield. But when I met him buying flowers in Camden Street one evening, it seemed a good moment to smile and say, 'How's Triona?'

He looked at me coldly and drawled, 'I haven't a clue.'

Passing the restaurant that night, I saw the flowers in a tall vase in the window. She had gone.

She was driven; she still needed excitement, trouble, as the boats needed locks to raise them in the canal. Without that, she couldn't live. I soon heard more of the affair with her boss: it had been exciting, but she had been out of control. Her voice faltered, she had a frightened look in her eyes; she said, 'Why do you think we do these things?'

'I don't know.'

She smiled again. Now it was over. She was back with Alex, the calm water of the canal. She said, 'Why don't you come over some evening?'

'I must,' I said.

'You always say that. You don't want to, do you?'

'Of course I do.'

She was in the charity shop, buying men's clothes: cord trousers, a tweed sports coat. When I saw them on Alex, he reminded me of her mannequin.

I didn't recognize him for a moment. His hair was grey, and I realized that he had been dyeing it for years. The house had changed too. A velux window, a raised ceiling of new rafters made even his old books and prints look bright. Hands clasped behind his back like the Duke of Edinburgh, he studied a print of her own, a Schiele nude. Over a single glass of wine he talked of the old days. After a couple more, Triona was talking of a day she had cycled into town to look for work as a model, but turned back at the art college gate. 'I was ashamed,' she said.

Alex smiled, nodded. 'That was natural then.'

'No, I was ashamed my tits were so small.'

Shaking his head, smiling again, Alex stood up. 'I'll get more wine.' He stopped at the door. 'Would you like some chocolate?'

Maybe the chocolate remark did it. As the front door closed, she pulled her dress open. 'What do you think?' Desire didn't come into it, I knew. It was a last spit in the face of the past.

She had found her limits, he had found his way home. They faded into the general scene like other neighbours, like other wrongs done. Standing at the window one day, looking out at a downpour blister the pavement white, gush from drainpipes and flow in shining sheets across the street, I thought of old neighbours who had passed on. I had come to know others, but not so well, and hardly noticed when they too passed out of sight – the small blonde woman no longer cycled by with the fat boy on the back carrier – but when I did notice, I missed them all the more. I was part of this place. When Alex approached one morning, he put a hand on mine as he spoke.

'Triona's not well. If you want to see her, you should call soon.' He said the word, 'cancer'. When I had finished work that evening I went over with some flowers.

The way he first took them into the kitchen and put them in water reminded me of that long-ago orderly world. The door of memory opened, it wouldn't close. As we went upstairs to a large bright bedroom, I remembered that it had once been her work-room. The bed was luxuriously double, with white soft pillows, white starched sheets. She was lying on it like a queen, the cover thrown back, her knees up, watching a bedside TV. She wore pearl-grey silk pyjamas. Her hair was cut short, which suited her. Her face had the yellow of an expensive suntan. Her eyes were bright, from morphine.

'Triona.' I said. 'You look great.'

'I sleep all day. You came at just the right time.' She put her arms behind her head, rested one leg sideways on a knee. Evening sunlight came in the window. There was a roof garden outside, a patch of gravel with a small olive tree in a big earthen pot.

'You've done a lot with it.'

'Alex is good like that.' She wriggled her toes in the gold beam of sun.

I knew that I wouldn't see her again, but I said it again. 'You look great.'

'Better light a candle anyway,' Alex murmured as we went downstairs.

'Who's her favourite saint?'

'Augustine? Remember his remark?' He gave a smile, keeping the good side out. 'Chastity, God, but not yet.'

I COULDN'T mention it then. It wasn't the right time. There never would be a right time, I knew. It will be always between us. I could feel it like the night air as we left the bar and crossed the car park and walked along the canal lit bright by traffic crawling bumper to bumper into town.

The Mermaid

I WENT UP to the club on Sunday evening and watched the end of a game. Jack was there, and Eddie, and afterwards we sat in the bar. Jack told us about his son. Eddie went on about his wife. Then Rogers joined us – I hardly know him but he included me in a round. Soon we were on that magical drink when everything grows clear and warm. He began to talk.

HE DEALT in dreams with lonely women. They had the dream already; all he had to do was listen. All the dreams were the same: love.

He met her at a party. Her name was Madeleine. She was French. She wore a white silk scarf; a thin cream pullover scarcely tautened by her breasts. Her hair was short, tinted. She was in her forties, he guessed. She danced badly, but at his age it was a relief not to dance, so they stood against the wall and talked. She had been living in the west of Ireland; she was interested in folklore.

He was tortured by beautiful women squeezing past.

Around midnight the older guests began to leave, the younger ones turned up the music and serious dancing began. Now it was too noisy to talk. He said he was going, and asked if she was going too. Her eyes were blank as she agreed. He felt sad as she appeared down the stairs wearing a wheat-coloured woollen poncho and a large white knitted peaked cap.

They walked through the dark cold streets to where she lived. There was something wrong about her, a stiff unease, but when she smiled her face was natural for a moment, like the glimpse of throat above her silk scarf. She talked of Sheela-na-gigs, pagan rites suppressed by the Catholic Church, feminine wisdom passed on by old women, and other things he had no interest in. Stragglers from an English hen party passed by: drunken girls in miniskirts and wedding veils, one of them waving a phallus-shaped balloon. Through their laughter, the clatter of their high heels on the cobblestones, Madeleine described a stone cross carved with dolphins she had seen in the west of Ireland. She was interested in writing about these symbols from ancient mythology taken over by the Church. At last, in a street running down to the river, she stopped outside a Georgian house. He wasn't disappointed when she didn't ask him in. He kissed her cheek, said they must meet someday.

'When?' Her face was bright.

'Some day I'm passing, I'll knock on your door.'

She didn't like that Irish casual habit. She preferred a phone call, even half an hour before. It was only good manners. She wrote her number down.

He still had dreams of fleshy, handsome, peaceful women. But he hadn't found any. He had some revenge in disappointing other women's dreams of love. He phoned, a couple of weeks later, one long afternoon. She invited him to her flat the next Saturday at 11 am. He couldn't remember when he'd had a date in the morning.

He rang the bell, her voice answered at once, and the street door was buzzed open. Inside, a woman was cleaning the hall. The lift smelled of lilac air freshener, its bright mirror walls reflected every failing in his face. From the top corridor windows there was a view across rooftops to the sunlit gentle shapes of the Dublin hills.

In daylight her brushed short hair seemed smooth as lacquer, her make-up was delicate and pale as the silk scarf about her throat. He stepped onto a carpet the colour of magnolia, so clean he felt he should take off his shoes. But he wasn't sure about his socks, so he sat at once on the couch, a taut white oblong. There were paintings on the walls that seemed good enough to be in public galleries. He admired a cubist nude, saying it had a look of Braque, and she said that an uncle had left it to her in his will. There was an air of money, and inherited good manners. She gave him a coffee-table book while she went to the kitchen – a galley of light wood and steel. The book was on pagan religions; he was admiring a bare-breasted Bacchante when she returned with a tray. He shut the book and helped her to set china on a small glass table. He felt a tension when she sat beside him on the couch.

She talked, he listened. Her mother had reared her in Paris; her parents had divorced when she was a child. Her mother still had love affairs, dramatic, like opera. Madeleine had worked as a model, then as a dress designer for a fashion house. She had lived with a man for years, then it had ended, everything of her old life had ended in a car crash. She had almost died. After that year in hospital, her life had changed from a physical to a spiritual one. That was why she had come to live in the west of Ireland. She rested her back against the couch.

Now he had to reply – nothing committal, but not too detached either. Her story wasn't the sort he was used to. He settled for banality with an intimate smile. 'How did you like the west?'

'The people seemed friendly at first, when you met them in pubs. But behind that I found them cold. You got so far, then that was the end of it. They never invited you to their homes.'

He agreed, saying that country people lived with their families. She said that Dublin seemed to be the same. He said the young were different, but at this age in life – he smiled again – most people had settled down in pairs. She talked of other cities she had lived in, where adults didn't just live between home and pubs. He wondered why she had left those cities, if her life had been any different before the crash. He said Dublin was partly a city and partly a provincial town.

The phone rang. She went to answer. He understood now the reason for her stiff-backed walk. She spoke in the same distant friendly tone she had used with him. Sitting down again she explained that a priest she knew was coming to visit. She went to Mass in his church. She pointed to a kitsch picture of the Virgin Mary he had given her. The doorbell rang, and she introduced a Father Declan. After ten minutes' chat with the smiling homely priest, he made some excuse and escaped.

He thought of her sometimes in the following weeks: her mended body, the loneliness that drove her from that elegant flat to sitting in churches and making friends with priests. He rang again, one wet summer evening, and as they talked she mentioned that she was writing a book. She asked if he would look at it, correct the English? Again he made an appointment to see her, this time in the afternoon.

She wore sleek black trousers, a silk white blouse with the top button open, without a scarf, and he noticed red marks like eczema on her neck. She sat beside him on the couch, at the glass coffee table, and they looked at her script. It was about mermaids, a hundred pages of handwriting in turquoise ink. There were a few references to learned sources on the last page. It looked like a schoolgirl's project.

'Have you been working at it long?'

'For years.' She explained that the mermaid was an image of sea water, of womankind, of life. She mentioned the myth of the lady and unicorn, then talked about mermaids again. They were all images of spiritual life, of nature and rebirth ...

It was a way of spending her lonely time. He pointed out a few small mistakes of idiom. As she smiled and her face grew bright, he sensed an energy in the tense body beside him; but he hesitated to put his hand on hers. He didn't know where it would lead. She was fragile. He felt that her whole body was raw-sensitive, that even a touch of his finger would leave a mark like the red eczema on her neck. He said goodbye to the quick fling he had been reaching for. He sat back and listened patiently.

She talked of the big world of fashion and money. She knew how that world worked. If she could get backing, her book about mermaids might make a good film. She had known film-makers in Milan, New York ... He knew she wouldn't get anywhere.

In the following weeks, when she phoned him or he phoned her, he heard of the latest hurt. She had met some film-makers, they had asked her to give them a storyboard. And she had. But nothing had happened. It was typical of Ireland. In Paris, if someone said he would call you, then he called ...

Wandering around town one day he came across a copy of Andersen's mermaid tale, and he sent it to her by post. She rang to thank him, then in the same distant friendly tone mentioned that she was leaving Dublin. He felt a small surprise at her independence. She had been to the country, to take photos of some stone carving of a mermaid, and had seen a cottage to let. It was a sign. She began talking of astrology, the stars that linked us to the universe ...

He felt relieved that she was leaving, and he rang more often to ask how things were. It was only right. She was having trouble with the removal firm, she was busy seeing her things packed in crates. He smiled at her carefulness. She answered stiffly, 'Things ought to be treated with the respect they deserve.'

When she was safely gone, he wrote to her. She replied soon after, with a photograph of her new home. As he had expected, it was no cottage: he glimpsed a peacock, a lawn running down to a river. She invited him to visit for the weekend.

She deserved to be treated with respect, he told himself as he drove down one autumn Friday evening. Wind was blowing through old trees along a lane that led to what looked like an eighteenth-century farmhouse. They sat in a big kitchen floored with varnished flagstones, warmed by a range, while outside the wind blew louder, and rain ran down small-paned windows set in thick walls.

She was happy there. It was the house she had always wanted. There were civilized neighbours who had already invited her to their homes ... As she talked, she showed him through big square rooms with low ceilings, and he admired her cubist nude, felt a shock again before the kitsch Virgin Mary. Her study was upstairs, the desk neatly filled by those turquoise handwritten pages, pasted with photos and photocopied pictures of mermaids holding mirrors, combing their hair, reclining on their scaled fish tails. She went on talking as she prepared the dinner. She had been back to Paris. Her mother wasn't well. Her sister was abroad, married to a diplomat. Their father didn't keep in touch. She lit a candle on the table, and they sat down.

She wore a patchwork jacket, beautifully stitched squares of red, yellow, green. There was a buttercup leaf on the butter, a basil leaf in the tomato soup … every detail was just right. He felt her waiting for some remark or sign that would show as precisely what his intentions were with her. He had no intentions. There were only so many times you could fall in love before the heart said *Lies* and refused to play the game any more. But when she looked at him across the candle flame, he smiled.

'You're good at living alone.'

'It's an acquired taste.' Her smile opened a little, like a door, revealing a little of the loneliness inside.

Gently leaning forward, he asked if she had met any Irishmen she liked. Yes, she had met someone, but he had been so vague. The last time she had seen him he was still aimless, drifting about. She took a single glass of wine from the bottle he had brought. From that and the candle and the intimacy of their talk, her face took on colour and grew bright. He leaned a little closer, but her voice began to rise. Her book on mermaids could have made a good film for television. And that man she had met, who hesitated about every-thing – what was wrong with him? What was wrong with Irishmen? Were they afraid of their priests? Of their mothers? Of themselves? Had they any minds of their own? All her French friends here said the same. You got so far, then the Irish withdrew …

He sat back from the table as her voice rose higher still. It was almost a cry. 'I haven't felt like a woman since I came here. In Paris, when a man asked me out, he made me feel … like a woman!'

She stopped, as if suddenly aware of her outburst. The wind was still blowing; he heard a peacock's scream. He offered to help with the washing up, and then with the drying. He glanced at an old timber-cased kitchen clock, and said casually, 'Is it that time?' She showed him to a guest room, on the ground floor.

There was delicate scented soap in a china dish, a white fleecy towel, even a bedside book. He turned out the light. All he wanted was the peaceful dark. But as he lay in bed he heard her moving about upstairs. Her room was above his. He heard her bed creak, then heard her get out and walk the floor again. She was upset? Her damaged back was hurting her? Or was she trying to tell him that she was awake, waiting for him? The pacing and creaking went on for almost an hour. At last there was silence. Exhausted, he fell asleep.

The wind had gone next morning, and the rain. She said she was going into town, shopping, but didn't invite him to come. She was still embarrassed by the previous night's outburst, he thought. He said he'd enjoy a stroll about the place. He felt pure relief as her car wheels cut through pools of rainwater down the lane. Walking about the yard, he saw her attempt at gardening: a bed of cream and dark-blue pansies beaten to the clay by the storm. Ripe apples rotted amongst nettles growing tall under a tree. The sun came out, and following the sound of a river he walked along the lane.

An old woman sitting outside a cottage greeted him Good-morning, and he stood for a moment to chat. He said he was staying with Madeleine, but the old woman didn't seem to know who he meant. She patted the bench, inviting him to sit. From her voice, she wasn't local. No, she was from Eastern Europe, she said. She talked about her life's adventures, the suffering she had seen in the war, how she had met her husband, the paths that had led to their coming together, and to settling in this corner of Ireland at last. In easy silence then they watched a spider appear in a web strung between two Michaelmas daisies growing by the porch. They smiled together as the little white daisy flowers trembled with the spider's movement. When he looked at his watch, he saw that two hours had passed, but he sat there enjoying the autumn sun and this spirited old woman's company.

It was afternoon when Madeleine appeared, walking stiffly down the lane. When she saw him, she stopped. He saw confusion, and anger in her face as she came up the cottage path. Ignoring the old woman, she stood before him and said – almost cried – 'I've been looking everywhere for you!'

The old woman smiled and invited her to join them. Madeleine stood, flustered, her forehead cleft by a frown. Like a spoilt child, he thought. Deliberately polite, he moved to make room on the bench, and she had to sit down. There was shame as well as anger in her eyes. He had gone too far, he knew. But he couldn't take any more. He left that evening.

That was the last time he saw her. He wrote of course, and she replied. She wrote to say that her mother was ill, that she was returning to Paris. He wrote to sympathize when her mother died. She wrote to say how much she liked being back in Paris, and described the job she had found in a small museum. She didn't put an address on her letter, but when he was in Paris the following summer he found himself walking along by the River Seine to where she worked. In the cloistered courtyard, looking at carved pieces of medieval stone made beautiful by time, he imagined that this was the sort of place where at last she would be at home. He asked for her at the desk, the attendant nodded vaguely, said the name was familiar, but thought that she had left.

He had done his duty, and felt relief as he escaped. But as he went down the sunny boulevard, eyeing the beautiful faces in the flow, he half-expected to see her appear – tense, hurt, waiting for a slight, waiting for love. She was there, somewhere. As he drifted with the crowd he felt he was being carried, farther than ever, out to sea, where there was no love, to her.

'THAT'S VERY SAD,' Jack said. 'I could nearly tell that to herself.'

Eddie said, 'Don't.'

'No, that'd be handing in your gun.'

97

'You can't hand in your gun.'

That was how they talked on Sunday evening, feeling better as they parted and went home to their wives.

In New York

HE HAD SPENT so much of his life scratching for a living that he found it hard to believe he had some money now. His daughter found it easier, and brought him to a hotel starred with bronze plaques in memory of famous residents. When he heard the price and began to bargain, she withdrew, embarrassed; stepping forward again when a deal was done. A tall, laconic black porter led them upstairs. It was like a return to the Sixties. A woman with long grey hair, a long flowery dress was watering potted plants in the corridor. The sound of old rock music, the scent of herb seeped from closed doors.

'You're in the tropics, enjoy yourself.' The porter showed him into a big shabby white high-ceilinged room.

Two windows looked out on New York. His daughter stood at one, her boyfriend at the other. Over their shoulders he tried to see his life from this new perspective: as a man approaching sixty, who had married and reared a family, had had a little success. Alone abroad he was always nervous, but his daughter's presence calmed him, as his wife's would. He needed his family, so he had always rebelled against family. When his daughter and her boyfriend had gone, he felt a flicker of the excitement he had as a boy when his parents went out for the evening – those rare occasions. Rooting about the room, as he used to at home, he found an abandoned painting cut in half in the wardrobe; and written in dreamy pencil above the washbasin mirror: *All things are Buddha things. Language is illusory* – just what he might have seen here thirty-five years ago. He looked at his old face in the mirror. He hadn't grown an inch. In his school there had been a tree whose bark had grown about an iron paling post until only the tip showed. If he had grown at all, he had grown like that, embracing his limitations.

IN THE EVENING they brought him out to an Italian restaurant where they ordered a pizza for three, as big as the small table. Like his wife, his daughter was vegetarian, and when he noticed the slices of salami he said as usual, 'I'll eat them.'

'It's all right.' She lowered her head, embarrassed again, and murmured, 'I'm eating meat now.'

'I'm glad.'

Her boyfriend smiled. 'We were wondering how we'd be able to keep up the lies for a week.'

'It's strange.' He looked at her. 'You're just the age I was when I came here.'

She listened patiently as he reminisced over the red wine. He had thought then that he could leave his past behind. For a short while he had felt like a snake sloughing its old skin. Then he had realized he had no new skin. He had cracked up and gone home.

His daughter smiled too. 'Welcome back.'

The New York he remembered was remote from the city they

walked through. Times Square was smaller, duller, than the neon jungle where he had lingered. Central Park was bigger and brighter, different from the glittering menacing place he had hurried past at night. In time he had learned to face the panics and elations of those days, and they had flown. Now they were like the sparrows, lovely and ridiculous, squabbling in the ivy below his hotel windows.

He was yanked back from his memories next day. They were in a shop, enjoying the pleasure of dithering between bottles of French wine and half-gallon jars of Californian at wonderful low prices, when his daughter's phone rang. It was his wife, calling from Ireland to say that their old friend Eileen had died. His daughter crying was suddenly like a child again; and her boyfriend, even as he comforted her. The evening meal in their Manhattan flat became an Irish wake as they drank and talked of Eileen: the Christmas Day they had brought her to a family party, where she had grown bored and stood outside the front door, ringing the bell until they left … Eileen was the last of the artists' wives. It was fitting they had heard of her death in a wine shop. Wilful, intelligent, a chain-smoking, drinking Irish Catholic, she had shown him the way into a wider world at home. He decided to cut his holiday short, change his ticket and go back for her funeral.

IT LEFT HIM one last day in New York. With his daughter and her boyfriend he visited the Met Museum, watched them walk hand in hand slowly, eagerly past two thousand years of masterpieces, as if admiring a wonderful landscape from a train. That was when he thought of Joe, an old friend now living in New York. Back at the hotel he looked him up in the phone book, hesitated, then called, and in a moment heard a voice direct from the past. It hadn't changed. Joe invited him to lunch, gave directions to his apartment in the aloof, smiling voice he remembered from school. His daughter gave him a map, and the sort of advice he had once given her, and then he set off on his own.

Eileen had been old, her death was natural. It was so long since he had met Joe that their meeting could mean little now. He strolled peacefully in the sunlight, sitting here and there to pass the time. In Union Square two stoned buskers, one with a drum, the other wearing a brown cloak and a plastic horned Viking helmet, pranced about the grass. A gay type cried, 'Horny bitch!' and he smiled. What had frightened him once, at best amused him now. Two sunbathing girls sat up and laughed as the buskers circled them in an obscene dance. He wandered on, down as far as Canal Street, allowing himself to get lost, asking directions and finding his way again. This was the life he had aimed at, fallen short of, and which his daughter was embracing now. He felt no bitterness. His life had grown in another direction, like that tree at school around the iron paling post.

JOE LIVED in the sort of shabby smart street he had once dreamed of: up-market, downtown bohemia. As he rang the bell he noticed a jazz bar next door – just right for Joe who had spent evenings long ago trying to win him over to Charlie Parker. The door was buzzed open and he was in a space before another door, of glass, which was buzzed open too. But – excited under his calm now – he missed it, and stood there trapped until Joe came down the stairs.

'That happens.' Joe gave his old smile.

His hair was white, but otherwise he was the same tall thin 1960s' schoolboy, his long fingers still bony and red. Talking, interrupting each other, they went up black-painted wooden stairs to a lofty apartment where Joe's wife embraced him and turned her cheek for him to kiss. He hardly knew her, only at the last minute retrieved her name, and said, 'Sally.'

He too was a Sixties' boy still. He felt disappointment at th neat rugs and paintings, the tidy shelves of books, including an effort of his own, the cushions on the sofa in a row. He had half-expected Joe to have cut himself dramatically clear of the past, but Joe had done what he himself had done: made an adult compromise. There were a couple of old prints of Dublin scenes from a set he remembered in Joe's parents' home. He smiled as he noticed, pinned to the kitchen memo board, an Irish postcard of silage bales daubed 'Feck off crows.'

That was the Joe he had known: a sniper, hiding downstairs in the kitchen from his deep-voiced, successful father. Joe had tried everything within bourgeois reason to escape the life his parents had seen as natural. He had dodged Law, tried Medicine instead, but had disliked that too. A working-class boy went to jail for a while, a country boy flogged the cattle and ran off to England, and a middle-class boy in those far-off days had a nervous breakdown. Joe had done his stretch in the desert of loneliness and confusion, then married Sally and gone to live abroad. They hadn't any children – a quiet *No* to that past, he thought.

He was a smoker still, so they sat outside in the sun on a timber veranda. Joe said he had given up cigarettes – another break from the past. Otherwise, Sally did the talking. She worked for a famous international firm, and mentioned by first name people he knew only from newspapers. He tried to include Joe, turning the talk back to the time when they had been close, but besides not sharing these memories Sally's role seemed to be centre-stage, and Joe seemed to prefer it that way.

Looking at her, he saw a resemblance to Joe's father: the same authoritative manner and heavy build. Joe had been closer to his mother; living with her when his father died; the curtains drawn in summer as they watched Wimbledon tennis, sharing their cigarettes; both insomniacs, comparing notes on their sleep. Sally had rescued Joe from all that, he thought.

She was looking at him now, like a teacher at an inattentive pupil. He nodded to show he was listening. She was talking about her mother's first meeting with Joe's mother.

'... They began to mention people they knew, and suddenly it was like – You know the Fitzgeralds too? – And straightaway they were on the same wavelength!'

She wasn't bright, he realized, or even confident. He tried again to nudge a way through her talk, asking Joe what he had been doing since they had last met. But Sally took over again, saying they had been in Hungary where her business had taken them. He finished his cigarette, and Joe brought him inside to see a picture they had bought in their travels. Sally stood behind him as he looked at a large painting of hobby horses in a merry-go-round. He didn't like it. It was like a mural for a fashionable bar. He turned to a smaller, unframed picture. 'That's good.'

'You gave it to us.' Joe's voice was dry.

'That's right, as a wedding present!' Sally said. 'A Charlie Parker, isn't it?'

'That's another Charlie.' Joe corrected her gently.

'His widow died yesterday,' he said, and explained that he was going home to the funeral.

But even as they talked of that, he saw annoyed embarrassment in Sally's eyes. She wasn't used to being wrong. That wasn't her role. She stepped forward, again taking over the conversation. They had a place in mind for lunch, it was just around the corner. 'You'll like it. It's *full* of books!'

'Well –' Joe's mild voice was almost self-mocking. 'Half-full.'

He went to the bathroom and washed his face in cold water. Sally was heavy going. He felt her presence even in the spotless mirrors and black marble counter. It had the look of a place where a maid – another shade from the past – came in. Tubes, bottles of make-up and perfume breathed the question: sex?

He looked at them as they went outside – Joe in a blue denim yachting cap, Sally in sunglasses – and tried to imagine them in bed; skinny Joe buried between Sally's big breasts. She interrupted this reverie, saying how much fun their street was, pointing out a drag queen, a gaunt stubble-jawed freak in a frock and high heels. He was afraid she was going to know the guy by name. She would have liked that. But she was too straight for that. But without her kind the world wouldn't work, he conceded as she led the way through a doorway in an old brick wall, across a courtyard, into a bar with a plank floor and wooden stalls. It was just the sort of place he liked, where good plain meals were served. He would never have found it on his own.

In his own eyes he was as mild-mannered as Joe, but he hadn't grown up without effort. Defeated in New York, hurt pride as much as confusion had driven him to fight back. His upbringing had failed him in the big world, and he had declared war on its limitations. He had found other friends, such as Eileen, who had shown him that there was security only in freedom.

Sally seemed nervous of him now, as if she sensed his reserve. She mentioned a public figure, a friend of hers, whom they had taken to dinner in this restaurant. He nodded and she went on, floundering in heartiness. 'Mary loved it – you know, she could shake off her shoes, say piss and fuck without anyone noticing!'

'I never noticed,' Joe said.

It was a normal complicated marriage, he thought. They defended each other. Sally provided the muscle, and in that shelter Joe's quiet confidence could grow; in turn protecting the other, soft side to her bluster, which no doubt she revealed to him, perhaps in bed.

She said the lunch was their treat; the beer turned out to be a good strong brew, and he warmed to her. She asked about his life. He said his wife was still in the same job, and he was still working at home.

'Just like us!' Sally smiled. 'Joe's face simply lights up when I leave in the morning!'

He didn't return the smile. The comparison implied they were the same, that he still lived in the world he and Joe had once shared. They had been close then because their problems had been the same: protected and repressed, afraid of life and women, they had huddled together like swallows on a wire before the inevitable migration.

He didn't want those days back – never, never – but they were all he had in common now with Joe, and he tried again to turn the talk back to that long golden sunset of boyhood when they had travelled across Europe by train. With Anthony, another school friend, they had visited Paris, Vienna, Athens, Istanbul, even the ruins of Troy. Joe didn't respond. He had forgotten, left behind, or wasn't able for those memories, and the dark drop that had followed. The conversation stalled. Sally, like a good hostess, took on the duty of starting it again.

'How's Anthony? Still hiding in the closet?'

'How do you mean?' He smiled, but raised his eyebrows coolly.

'Well – single and fifty-eight …?' Sally laughed. 'He's gay, obviously!'

'He always has a girlfriend.'

'Camouflage!' Sally laughed heartily again.

'I wouldn't mind some of that camouflage. His latest girl's a 29-year-old Japanese.'

Sally backed down, but she had lost face and had to make it up. She began talking about her high-flying job, but it reminded him of a golf-club lady beaten to a parking space, accelerating blindly to find another. She was used to being right. That was the deal. She maintained the high privet hedge and black spearhead railings of Joe's old suburban home.

That was where his irritation was coming from. He hadn't had Joe's bourgeois inheritance to help, or hinder him. He had run out of it straight to New York, cracked up and gone home, and after his own journey through the desert had married and settled down. His life seemed suddenly a mirror image of Joe's. His irritation became cool anger. He waited quietly, let Sally advance. She began talking about South Africa, where she was going next week to oversee some training programme.

'What's the programme?'

'We're training the junior staff, local people we're training to take over.'

He remembered that we-know-better voice from the past. He was able for it now. He nodded. 'What will they be doing?'

'It's a training pack we're having printed.'

'You're bringing the training pack with you?' He sprinkled a little salt on the side of the plate.

'Yes, they'll take over then. It's very simple.'

'That's what you were doing?'

She blundered on. Finally she was silent. He glanced at her deep-set tired eyes, the brown slack skin beneath them. She put a good face on her defeat, asked for the bill and insisting on paying. As she signed a MasterCard slip she said, 'I'm sure you and Joe have lots to talk about. I have to go to my office.'

He hadn't had any wish to hurt her. He had been defending himself, the little freedom he had won. Calm again, he kissed her cheek goodbye.

Now he and Joe were free to talk, but they were silent as they strolled the sunny streets. He suggested sitting down, and Joe led the way to a bench in a small sandy, tree-shaded square. He lit a cigarette. 'What are you doing with yourself?'

Joe did a Cockney accent, as he had long ago. 'I do a bit o' writing, myself.'

'Anything published?'

Joe shook his head.

'What do you write?'

'Plays, mostly.'

'Any performed?'

Joe shook his head again.

'Why not? Have you tried?'

There was a glint of steel in Joe's boyish smile. He backed down. Joe glanced at his cigarette. 'What are they?'

'They're not bad. Turkish.'

'I sometimes smoke the odd one ... outside.'

Sally had banned smoking, and Joe was signalling for help? Having a little rebellion? Making an effort at intimacy? He handed him a cigarette. The way Joe drew on it deeply reminded him of that long-ago intensity, the desperate innocence of their high-spirited talk as freedom had drawn close; a night in an Austrian bar when they had silently watched workmen at the next table drive pins into their powerful arms, challenging each other's endurance. Joe breathed smoke slowly down his nostrils, then dropped the cigarette on the sand, half-finished. 'What would you like to do?'

He thought it was some great question, but Joe meant simply that. They wandered down the street to a vast bookshop, where he looked for a present to bring home. He felt a small shock as he saw Joe lost in a book, shutting it reluctantly as he approached. Already Joe was returning to his own world.

'Would you like to meet my daughter?' That was the best he could manage.

'Sure.'

Together they walked to her flat, not far, but their silence made it seem endless. When he rang the bell, she came downstairs with her boyfriend. The owner of a music shop next door stepped out onto the pavement and they chatted gratefully with him for five minutes more. Then it came down to small talk.

'When are you going back?'

'Tomorrow.'

His daughter picked up the silence. 'Would you like to come in?'

Joe looked at his watch, gave his aloof self-mocking smile, and turned away. 'I must go back to my Sally.'

He wanted to run after him, suggest a drink, in a bar try again for that past togetherness. The blue yachting cap disappeared into the crowd. He grasped at images – *All things are Buddha things* – the paling post enfolded in the old tree's bark. But the facts were that he was going back to Ireland, and Joe was staying in New York.

Kestrel and Starlings

ALMOST ALL THE MEN in the townland had the same name, but in different forms – Paddy, Páraic, P.J., Pak – so you hardly noticed they were the same. You noticed it in the graveyard on the hill when you saw the full name on each headstone. Some houses had a statuette of Saint Patrick set into their gate pier, but if it was smashed by a tractor or a delivery lorry reversing it wasn't replaced. The few young men left were busy all day. Each small farm had its own small advantage and disadvantage: a stream or a well, and some wet land; or some good land on an awkward slope.

They were shy. If a man saw a stranger come up his boreen, he might step back into his house and wait until there was a knock before coming to the door. They were used to hearing their accent imitated by comedians on TV. They didn't often visit each other, but when they passed on the road they stopped and rolled down their car windows and talked until another car moved them on. To fall out with someone was terrible; someone with the same name, whose father lay beside your father up in the graveyard, whose great-grandfather had helped your great-grandfather build his house — whom you had to pass on the road now without talking, every day, maybe forever, until you lay side by side up in the grave-yard under the same full name. So they were tolerant — of moodi-ness and oddness, drinking, not shaving, bachelor clothes and untidy homes. In winter they often vanished from each other's sight for months. They no longer went to work in England or America, but that memory had made them casual with long absence. When Marcus appeared they just said, 'You're down again.'

HE HAD BEEN GIVEN a name in keeping with the new life his parents had made in the city, but as a boy on summer holidays this poor farm had been his second home. As a young man he had hardly visited, but it had always been at the back of his mind. What he had seen down here — an owl blundering from an ivied tree in daylight ... fallen ash leaves plastered on the wet road — remained clear of daily habit, as fresh as when he had seen it first. By middle age this place had become as an image of certainty, a fixed point. But when his uncle died and left it to him, he was shocked. It had meant so much to him that he feared to see it now. He drove down from Dublin with his wife one weekend, to look at it and decide what to do.

The first glimpse, through a lank hedge as he came around the bend of the narrow road, was another shock: the 1950s' bungalow, the field spattered with rushes at the foot of the small hill. It seemed to be in a hole. Failure, isolation, the grip of the past — all the fears he had gathered since boyhood sprang up. The boreen was overgrown, his car skidded over sheets of lodged wet grass. His shoulder caught a blackthorn branch, and cold raindrops showered on his head. He breathed in the raw silence, the rank sweet elderflower smell. When he opened the door it caught on an ESB bill. The envelope was damp. The ashes in the hearth were sodden by rain that had come down the straight wide chimney. Wind rumbled under the slates. But when the fire was lit and he looked out the big kitchen window, down over hedges to the silver flash of the lake and the blue shapes of the sea-coast mountains far beyond, he felt peace.

All his deepest delights had been here. His city home had been shadowed by his father's long struggle to succeed. This place had meant wild freedom – his uncle holding a mug of tea under the mare to whiten it with her milk. He remembered her sweat-wet flanks stuck with hayseed, the green-foamed mouth and bared teeth as the bridle was caught and she was backed between the shafts after dinner for more work; the hedge trembling as she drew the heavy blue and orange cart; the crunch and roll of the iron-shod wheels down the sand road, the snap of the leather rein-ends on her rump, the bone-shaking trot, the crack of horse farts, the tail pluming up and the smell of falling gold dung …all day until the long sleep under blankets that smelled of turf smoke.

When he woke in the morning his wife was sitting up in bed, reading. He watched her put down the book and look out the window. A white butterfly was flitting about tall nettles that nodded above the sill. He sat up beside her and watched the butterfly rest on a leaf, its wings closed, its body curved underneath.

'What's he doing? Does he drink from the flowers?'

'It's a she. She's laying her eggs.'

When they had dressed they went outside, and he lifted a leaf to show her the pale-green eggs fixed like tiny rivets underneath. She laughed with wonder and turned her face to the sun, opening her arms as if for an embrace. 'Oh lovely light.' She closed her eyes and swayed from side to side. That was why he had married her.

She was good. She had put up with his dreaming and wandering, and now they were home. He felt that boyhood peace again.

She came from another world; this place meant nothing to her. She knew nothing of the yellow nettle-roots she dug, that turned and rooted in the clay again, and in days sent up fresh stinging leaves. Like him she tossed them on the thorn hedge to wither, and pulled dock leaves to soothe the white blisters the stings raised. They worked all morning, and had their lunch of milk and sandwiches outside. The breeze blew through the sally bushes along the ditch, lifting their leaves, showing the pale grey underneath. As naturally, quietly, they lay down together in the wild grass: he stamping his mark on this childhood home, she gathering his strange adult peace into herself. They slept then until rain fell warm and heavy on their face, but they lay there for a minute more, watching a frog, green-gold, motionless, in the damp roots before they went into the house. The peace there was like the peace he felt inside. The disorder – a sheep clippers, a rusted tin of beans, a bag of sugar like a rock on the table – only made clear the simple pattern of his uncle's life.

'He never married?'

'No. I'd say Paddy died a virgin.'

Her face filled with wonder, as it had at the butterfly's eggs.

'That was the way then.'

The gutters trickled into silence, the sun appeared between dark slate clouds, tinting the ash-tree branches silver, and they sat outside against the warm bonnet of the car.

'What will you do with it?'

'I don't know.'

He rooted his toe under a rotting green hose pipe, she stooped and drew it up, and together, tearing it free of matted grass, they followed its snaking to a cattle trough full of dead leaves. A tractor roared down the narrow road, and they set to work again. In a few days her face was bronzed, and his was red. She had a mix of blood, he was the freckled Celt.

SHE CAME IN SUMMER, as he had once come, but in winter he came alone. One snowing day when fire could not spread, he dragged his uncle's rotten furniture out into the field, threw on a can of petrol, lit a match and ran. He kept the long kitchen table of planks worn into ridges, the clumsy deal chair, the stool smudged with faded blue cart paint, and his uncle's old canvas armchair. He painted the walls pale and the ceilings white. Each time he came, he sharpened his uncle's worn scythe with the broken whetstone and mowed the grass and rushes about the house. As he walked the clean field in the evening and breathed its sweet scent, he had that childhood peace again.

Sometimes it lasted for days. The damp green moss six inches deep on the ditch banks, the red spongy moss in the cutaway bog, the huge bleached stones in the small walls about the small fields – they hadn't changed. The crest of wild grass still grew in the centre of the road. A mare, maybe a granddaughter of his uncle's wild mare, sank on her haunches to stale, and the wind blew the piss to spray. He walked the thin tar road around the townland, chatting with his uncle's old neighbours, but his life and theirs were different. He was just a city visitor, restless after a few days. But before he left he always stood for a minute as he shut the gate, looked up the trim boreen at the smoke of the last embers rising from the chimney, the pheasant already advancing from the thorn hedge to peck in the mown field. It was a shrine to peace.

NATURE PRESSED IN. A boundary bank was knocked by accident, then another one. Furze crawled over the hill. To keep the land, he planted it with trees: ash, alder, beech, larch, pine, sweet chestnut, oak. Their children joined them for a week each summer, beating down the briars and nettles until the saplings had risen into the light. But still there was the house. When he arrived in winter the walls and windows were glistening with cold damp. Wind carried slates away and the roof leaked. The rushes grew in spring, green briars snaked out from the hedge. His drive west became more duty than pleasure. His wife came less often in the summer: her nature was giving, growing attached to people; not holding on to a place far away. But still he couldn't bring himself to sell. In the end, ambivalent, he let the house. It was a year before he returned to see how the tenant was getting on.

THE BOREEN was worn to mud, the overhanging blackthorns had been hacked away, sacks of coal were heaped against the gable he had painted white. It was like any poor country bungalow. He heard TV noise, a child crying inside. She had the child in her arm when she opened the door. The porch was full of turf, sticks, a bush saw, a Calorgas cylinder – everything was to do with keeping warm. She shut each door behind them and shoved a mat against the door. A clothes line hung from the kitchen ceiling, the cement floor was carpeted and littered with toys. A small boy sat on the clumsy deal chair looking at a TV on a shelf her husband had fixed to the wall. It was just what he had wanted it to be, a living house. She sat in his uncle's old canvas armchair, took a joint from the hob and lit it, as naturally as his uncle had lit his pipe. The hot rich scent of herb mixed with turf smoke and made a strange new scent.

He was too close to this country to stand out. When he talked with the neighbours his voice slipped into their tone. He had been careful not to be caught at sunset mooning over a blackbird's song. She was different, herself. When the neighbours found her sitting on a ditch, cross-legged, and asked was she all right, she answered simply, 'I'm doing my yoga.' They were polite, and only said that she was odd. She walked the road in her long tweed overcoat, talked in her plain middle-class voice about children's allowances or the Offenbach she had heard on Lyric fm. She invited the neighbours' children in for drawing lessons, talked to them about the left and right sides of the brain, told them to draw whatever came to mind. She had hung green scapulars in one of the hawthorn trees; tiny Buddhist bells in another tinkled with the wind. When he saw the parlour mirror ruined by rain behind the cart house, she explained that she didn't want to see herself. To make herself plain, she had cut her long hair short as a boy's. But she was beautiful still. She boiled a kettle, poured green tea leaves like pine needles into the teapot. She had a Brennan's sliced pan, but also anchovies. She sat down, opened a blue plaid shirt, bared a white breast and nursed the baby as they talked. He looked away, up at his uncle's mildewed picture of Our Lady of Good Counsel that she had left on the kitchen wall.

SHE HAD BEEN the only one to answer his advertisement. Unerring fate had found the right tenant for this shrine to peace. Her husband was out at work all day; she was at home living a childhood dream. Each time he called he saw it drift closer to a nightmare. The shed was too far from the house, she had the turf tipped at the gable, and soon it was too wet to burn. The wild grass went on growing, the rushes drew closer, nettles were nodding their heads again above the windowsill. Ivy he had trained against the wall began to creep over the windowpanes. Her husband began to spend more time in the pub, and soon he was drifting away. When the ivy closed over the back door, she left suddenly and moved into a nearby cottage with central heating. He had to drive down again to an empty house.

WITH A CLAW HAMMER he tore the ivy from the back door. The field behind was a wilderness. The scythe wasn't able for three years of grass and rushes; he asked a neighbour to sweep the field with a mowing machine. He said that he was preparing it for sale. But when he walked the field that evening and saw a rabbit chopped in half among the sweet swathes, he changed his mind again. He couldn't do it. He couldn't sell.

He was sitting by the fire when he heard a knuckle knock on the front door. It echoed through the empty house, and then she stepped inside with the child in her arms. She had allowed her hair to grow again; it lay about her shoulders, thick auburn gold. She sat in his uncle's canvas armchair, as naturally as if she still lived there, and they talked. Her husband had gone; their marriage was over, now she was living alone.

The child fell asleep in her arms, and they talked more quietly. She missed this place already, she said, its air of peace. He agreed. He said he had often called on his uncle, as unexpectedly as she had called now, and found him in that canvas armchair, his feet on the stool, looking up at the ceiling or at the fire. He had once asked him what he thought of as he sat there, and his uncle said, 'Musha nothing, dreaming.' He had once asked if he was happy, and his uncle had said, 'Why wouldn't I?' as if he had been asked was he alive. He had even asked once if he was afraid of dying, and his uncle had said, 'Why would I? Isn't very near everyone I know dead.'

They talked about him as they sat by the fire. He had lived in this place for ninety-two years, except for one season in England working on a farm. He had never set foot in Dublin, never married, never been ill, never known a holiday. She said that that was beautiful. He agreed again. The evening light, reflected from the grass growing up to the window, threw a green glow into the room. She sank lower in the armchair, her body slackened by tiredness, intimacy, warmth. Then it was dusk, but they went on talking, their stretched feet a foot apart. In the firelight he saw her face dissolve until it was like the sleeping child's. She answered his look with a smile of dreamy desire. It would take a moment, said a butterfly thought, to take the child from her arms, lie it to sleep in the canvas armchair, and lead her into his uncle's bedroom. But he couldn't do that. That mass of memories was too strong, that dream of peace blocked the door.

IT DREW HIM BACK. Again nature was advancing, resolute now. A tendril of ivy worked in above through the warped frame of the kitchen window, and grew up the pale painted wall. Field mice squeezed underneath the door. Jackdaws dropped sticks down the chimney, and would continue until one lodged. A storm lifted the roof from the turf shed and blew it across the field like a hat. The silence took on a life of its own; at night it seemed to move out from the walls into the centre of the room. One night a fox's laughing mask appeared at the dark window, and for half a minute held his stare. To get out one evening, he went for a walk, along the thin tar road, down by the wind-crushed hawthorns, down to her new home.

IT WAS ON A STEP of a steep hill. Its door opened onto the road. Children's toys lay on the roadside, there was road grit inside on the floor. There was a piano, a brindled greyhound she had rescued from Travellers, and a boxer dog that a divorced friend had given her to mind. His eyes followed her as she moved about the kitchen, tidying while she talked. She was pregnant – she was with someone else now; she was the talk of the townland, she smiled. Cattle roared from a slat house nearby. He gave money to the children, and looked at their school homework. They couldn't remember his name. When they reminded their mother that they were going shopping to Lidl, he stood to leave. As she searched for her car keys and put up the fireguard, she said an absent goodbye. The moment they had shared in green twilight was scattered, like the toys on the side of the road.

As he continued down the steep hill he saw her daughter's Hello Kitty purse on a stone wall, soaked, with a few cents rusting inside. Crossing the wall, he walked down through sedge grass already stiffening with frost. Memories hung in every hawthorn, like her green scapulars and Buddhist bells. He remembered when there had been a lake there, where in winter the old men had hunted for pike; walking on the ice with a sledge hammer, striking when they saw a shape below; smashing open the ice then and drawing out the stunned fish. The lake had been drained, there was only a stream now, winding through a bed of white marl. The old men had said that long ago, before the lake was there, the Fianna had raced their horses on this plain ...

There was a rasping cry; two snipe flew from the rushes, zigzags of silver and brown. As he stood to watch them he heard a shrill chattering, and saw a migrant flock of starlings settling for the evening in the trees about the ruined big house. They rose suddenly like a swarm of bees, and he saw a kestrel gliding towards them – sickle wings and long straight tail, like a small anchor in flight. With a rushing sound like wind in trees the flock closed tight. The kestrel turned away, and the flock scattered. He heard the sound of their wings, like a fire burning overhead.

He stood in the cold air, watching as the kestrel returned, copper against the dark cloud. The long skein of birds drew into a black ball. Now it was a sound like a furnace burning, a quiet roar. The kestrel flew into its centre, which shattered open like a thousand broken pieces when he passed through. A fourth attempt followed, and again they made a hedgehog ball, into which he plunged. Again he appeared from the other side without prey. They dropped suddenly behind the old island, a thicket of alder trees in the lake bed, to shelter until it was dark. He heard the whistle of a bird or an otter, then a squeal like a rabbit's, as he walked back to the road.

Her car had gone, the door was shut, the greyhound and boxer were lying outside. She was learning what it was to live all the year in this place. He had always been a visitor like the starlings, flying from its grip, always coming back — for what? As he left the Hello Kitty purse on the windowsill he saw the fire burning quietly inside, a red glow in the dark. The dogs snarled, and he turned away. They lay down at the door again, watching as he walked up the dark steep hill. At last he had made up his mind. He would spend one last night in his uncle's house. He would go into town next morning and see the auctioneer.

Mister Pock

IT'S LATE, 11.30 at night. It's raining, the first rain in a month. Both windows are wide open still, it's been so warm. He can hear the rain falling in the back garden, rattling on the privet trees. He can see their cream blossoms even in the dark. The sweet scent comes even through the rain. Then he hears a groan. Standing up, he looks out at the dark backs of the houses in the next street. It comes again. It's like the sound of another species. It's been so long since he was a part of that, it's a while before he realizes what it is. His wife goes on reading, he goes on writing his letter. It goes on for five minutes more. There's a boy's cry, and at last it's over. A light comes on, and a girl's face appears at an open window, leaning out smoking a cigarette.

AFTER THIRTY YEARS living in this street he sees it through the glass of time. When the young couples leave their doors open these summer evenings, he sees not just their pale sanded floorboards but the carpeted front rooms of the people who lived there before. There's a story in every house. The derelict garage door is black because Mr Campbell came out one morning, sweating, in a miniskirt, with a pot of paint, and covered it with white zigzags. They took him away. The black cat is watching Delia's house because she gives him food.

He's been here so long he remembers the beginning of that story, a few street cats slowly growing wild. They hunted the canalbank reeds for ducklings; waited under cars for street pigeons to land. At night he heard them on the rooftop, running down the alley after rats. When his children were small they had tried to tame one, lured it inside at last and shut the door. That was when they saw what wild meant – spitting, screaming like a firework, throwing itself against the window until they set it free. He saw it on the back garden wall one evening crouched under a tom, and the next year a wild litter was born. And the next. One winter night he saw a dozen of them, a black inbred pack, hunting in the snow. A neighbour called the Corporation, who came and trapped a few. Others left for better territory. In the end there was only this one. He waits until the door has shut, then advances slowly. The thick lace curtain opens and Delia appears at her front window to watch him eat.

AND NOW THERE IS the new face that appears at the back window – young, golden-brown, in a frame of oiled black hair. If she weren't so tall she could be from the Philippines. Maybe South America, he thinks. When he goes down for the milk and paper in the morning, she is coming round the corner, setting out for work. She doesn't walk on the pavement but in the middle of the street, along a straight black seam of tar. He notices her springy breasts, her pale tight blue jeans, her bottom twitching like the waterhen's white rump when it runs down the canal bank from the cat.

One day going past the restaurant, he sees her inside cleaning the big window. As she reaches up to spray the top half with an aerosol he sees her bared brown stomach, a jewel swinging from a gold navel ring. He smiles at her but she looks through him, as if he were a windowpane.

HE GIVES the same glance to old Delia. She reminds him of what's ahead. Usually he walks past with a word about the weather, but now she has a pretext. 'You didn't see Mister Pock?'

'Who?' He has to stop.

'The cat. That's what they do call him.'

'He was in our garden yesterday, he killed a sparrow.'

'Well did he?' Seeing his look, she withdraws. 'Well isn't he terrible.'

Her wirrastrue country accent, the *Maria* wooden plaque screwed outside her door – everything about her gets on his nerves. He is about to slip away, but she says, 'You wouldn't open a tin for me. That tin opener, it's as stiff.'

She can't go upstairs any longer, her bed fills the front room. A Sacred Heart picture hangs over the fireplace, the heating is on full blast, Daniel O'Donnell is on the TV crooning a song. As soon as he opens the tin of Whiskas he almost runs out the door. But a threshold has been crossed. Now each time he passes he has to stop and talk. Her big lonely eyes fix on his. He can't escape.

So he remembers how it happened, he knows how it was done. He's at her doorstep talking when the cat comes around the corner, belly slung low, yellow-green eyes with black-slit slanted pupils looking left and right. It's the first time he's been so close to him, he sees his black coat is flecked with white hairs. Delia smiles, and he rubs his side against the lamppost, then he brushes against her legs. 'Well, Mister Pock,' she says. 'Are you going to come in?'

She goes inside, leaving the door open. The cat glances over his shoulder, then slowly steps in.

AS HE'S GOING down the street one morning, her door opens and Mister Pock slips out. Delia blushes like a girl when she sees him. He glimpses her bare feet, a pink nightdress as she withdraws. But another threshold had been crossed. Soon she is ringing him at night.

'Well, were you looking at the *Late Late*?'

'I missed it,' he says.

'Indeed you didn't miss much. They had this fella with long hair on talking for half an hour. Now, Pat, I said to myself, if you've any sense you won't argue with him. That's just what he wants ...'

He doesn't answer one night. An hour later the blue flashing light of a squad car stops outside her door. Two guards go in. He rings when they have gone.

'What happened? Are you all right?'

'I couldn't open the tin, and I said to myself, I'll ring Kevin Street. Well they were nicest lads – and do you know what, one of them is from Ballindine. Delia, they said, do you mean to say that the neighbours wouldn't do that for you?'

'I'm sorry.'

'Delia, they said, it's no trouble in the wide world. Any time you want, just pick up the phone, they said.'

'Don't,' he says. He has to. 'Ring me.'

SHE RINGS in the evening, as soon as they turn on the light. 'It's only me.'

'How are you?'

'Well I'm that worried, I couldn't sleep a wink. I haven't seen Mister Pock these two days.'

'I'll keep an eye out for him.'

'You couldn't have a look now?'

He can't refuse the timid weak voice, he can't fight back. With the phone to his ear he walks around the corner, and down the next street. He finds him lying under a hedge in a neat front garden beside a fat ginger cat.

'He's here.'

'Oh thanks be to the Sacred Heart. Where?'

'Right beside me.'

'Pock –' she begins, and he holds the phone through the railings. Pock bares his stained brown teeth and draws back. 'Pock, do you hear me? Do you know what I'm after buying for you? A bit of chicken ...'

The fat ginger cat slides out through the railings. Mister Pock follows at her tail. He hears their mating screams from the derelict garage roof that night.

SHE RINGS as usual when their light comes on. He kicks the wall savagely, then picks up the phone. 'How are you?'

'Musha, only middling.'

His kick leaves a mark in the plaster. He kneels down and rubs it clean. 'How's Mister Pock?'

'Look at him, lying on the bed like a lord. Do you know what, I think he only comes here when it suits him.'

'You don't need anything?'

'Well that's what I was going to ask you. You wouldn't feed himself while I'm away?'

'Where are you going?'

'They say I have to go into hospital.'

'When?'

'Tonight, they said. You wouldn't come over, and I'll give you the food.'

She hardly ate any longer. Her legs are as thin as her walking stick. He says, 'You should get the Meals on Wheels when you come home.'

'Indeed I tried that. Sure it's not food at all.'

'And what would you like?'

'Do you know what it is, I think there's nothing nicer than a nice new potato.'

'Why don't you try that?'

'Well God knows you're right ...' She turns to a cardboard crate full of cat food. 'What he likes is the liver-flavour Whiskas, mixed with rusks. Isn't that right, Pock?'

'Don't worry about him.'

Pock slides from his armchair and springs onto her lap. From there he sticks out his small pink tongue, as if to say fuck off. He'd like to, but he sits and listens as Delia talks on and on. It's only right.

She came from a village in Mayo. Her parents died when she was young. She worked in a hotel in Dublin, and with her savings bought this small house ... He sees that everything about her is valiant. He still wants to run out the door.

'And then you came along ...' She tries to lift the cat with her bird's-feet hands. He's too heavy. She stoops to kiss him instead. She begins to cry when the doorbell rings. He slides from her lap when the taxi man comes in, then walks in a slow circle, rubbing against his legs. The man takes her suitcase and goes out to the car.

'You'll look after him, won't you?' Her voice is piteous, tears trickle down through the wrinkles in her cheeks.

He says, 'I will. '

HE'S SQUATTING on his haunches, pouring rusks into the plastic bowl. And who comes by? The beautiful girl. She stops when the cat walks around her, rubbing his side against her legs. Even standing still she is moving all the time – her hands, head, eyes, hips – restless, natural, eager, in a way that reminds him what youth is. She is like blossom the day it opens, stiff as the stem, rippling as if in a breeze. She makes him want to shine, but not to show off. She makes him want to be worthy of life, to be noble somehow.

She asks about the old woman he minded. He says she's gone into hospital. He asks where she comes from. She says Uruguay. He asks what is the capital of Uruguay. She says Montevideo. He thinks this could go on all day. He says he thinks the Irish used to emigrate to Montevideo. She says now it's the other way round, and he feels the force of her shining smile. It won't have weariness, it won't accept déjà vu. He can no more leave it than go indoors from the spring sunlight. She says she sees him from her window, she asks is he retired. He says he sees her working in the restaurant – and then he makes a mistake. To keep the conversation going, to go on breathing the scent of her youth, he asks what her boyfriend does. She says she doesn't have a boyfriend – there's an eye blink's pause, and he sees her realizing what he meant. As she walks up the street along the straight black seam of tar, he knows she won't speak to him again. He's made a mistake.

WHEN DELIA DIED she was brought back to her village and buried. Her house was put up for sale. Everything – the Sacred Heart picture, the Welcome doormat, the lace curtain – was thrown out into a skip. That was a year ago but the cat comes up the street every morning, belly swinging low, yellow-green eyes glancing left and right. There are saucers and dishes outside a dozen doors now – meat, chicken, milk, fish – all for Mister Pock. He springs onto a parked car's bonnet, lies on the sun-warmed metal, springs down and chases his shadow, dabs a paw at a blowing leaf. The young couples stroke him, he rubs his side against their legs, rolls onto his back. They walk away slowly, looking over their shoulders, calling. He follows for a few yards, then stops. The old writer and his wife leave their door open, but he won't go in. He won't enter any other house. He looks across the street at Delia's window and cries, piteously.